"It's my first Christmas without my family. I don't know how I'll get through it."

His voice cracked, and then was finally, blessedly silent.

She was silent for so long, and yet her silence was not uncomfortable. It was not her lips he was noticing now, it was her eyes. There was something in the dove-gray of those eyes that a man could hold on to, if he let himself.

"I know how you'll get through it." And then, unpredictably, she took a step forward, reached up on her tiptoes and kissed him. The kiss was a mere brush of her lips, butterfly wings against the petals of a flower. It was every bit as sweet as he had thought it would be.

And so much more that he was shocked. Her lips, smooth, silky, soft, had touched his for less than a full second, and yet he felt rocked, as if an earth tremor had moved through his world. He felt the walls he had built around himself so diligently— brick after careful brick—shift slightly, dangerously.

"Maybe," she said softly, her voice a balm and a caress, "you have more to give than you think. And that's how you'll get through it."

Dear Reader,

In my early childhood my family was poor. Not so poor that we didn't have food or a home, but poor enough that I knew better than to ask for the shiny red shoes or the brand-new two-wheel bicycle. I loved Santa Claus because I felt free to ask him for that secret, silly, frivolous thing I coveted.

That love continues to this day, when I am able to select a few tags off the community Santa tree. The children I buy gifts for never know who I am, and I never know who they are. How can such a small, anonymous act cause a feeling almost too large to hold within the human heart?

I know each of you has your own personal way of giving, so, from one Secret Santa to another, I wish you all the joy this season can hold.

Cara Colter

If you'd like to share what you do to make Christmas special for someone, please contact me at my Web site, www.cara-colter.com.

CARA COLTER

Their Christmas Wish Come True

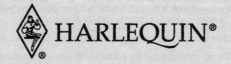

HARLEQUIN®

TORONTO • NEW YORK • LONDON
AMSTERDAM • PARIS • SYDNEY • HAMBURG
STOCKHOLM • ATHENS • TOKYO • MILAN • MADRID
PRAGUE • WARSAW • BUDAPEST • AUCKLAND

ISBN-13: 978-0-373-03983-8
ISBN-10:   0-373-03983-2

THEIR CHRISTMAS WISH COME TRUE

First North American Publication 2007.

Copyright © 2007 by Cara Colter.

Printed in U.S.A.

Cara Colter and her real-life hero, Rob, live on an acreage in a lush mountain valley in British Columbia. In true Canadian style, Cara shares her backyard with bears, coyotes, elk, deer, wild turkeys and the occasional moose. When not writing, Cara can be found enjoying her home (built by Rob), her garden or any one of eleven horses. She also has a very bossy cat, and a serious addiction to high-quality chocolate. Cara loves to hear from readers, and you can contact her or learn more about her through her Web site, www.cara-colter.com.

Don't miss Cara's next book from
Harlequin Romance®, on sale in February

The Playboy's Plain Jane

Opposites attract in this fun and fabulous story!

To my friend, Doreen Cardwell

CHAPTER ONE

Forty days until Christmas…

THE doorbell ringing sounded like a cannon going off, the balls landing and exploding inside his own head.

Michael Brewster groaned, rolled over, pried one eye open and looked past an empty beer bottle, lying on its side, to his bedside alarm clock.

Six o'clock. Morning or evening? Morning. Who the hell would call on him at six in the morning? He pulled a pillow over his head, but the door chimed again, and then again. Groggily, grumpily, like a bear coming out of hibernation, he groped over the side of his bed, found a pair of jeans and pulled them on.

Bare-footed and chested, he stumbled down the hallway and threw open his front door. The bracing November air cleared his head, and he reluctantly bit back his temper.

His neighbor, Mr. Theodore, stood there, wizened as a little elf, looking impossibly cheerful given the early hour and the fact that the sky was a dark, leaden gray behind him, promising a grim day.

"Top of the morning to you, Michael."

With his head thudding and his mouth feeling as if he'd cleaned toilets with his tongue the night before, Michael wanted to snap at the old man and slam the door. But how could he?

Michael had recently moved back to the home he'd grown up in, and Mr. Theodore was part of the treasured memories that had drawn him back here, to the house that still smelled of his father's pipe. Michael and his brother, Brian, had raided Mr. Theodore's garden and picked his carefully tended flowers for their mom. They had broken the branches of his crab apple tree while climbing it, and played Halloween pranks on him.

Despite that history, or maybe because of it, Michael had felt initial wariness when Mr. Theodore had approached him about working around his house. A carpenter by trade, Michael was financially in a position where he never had to work again.

Besides, by saying yes, would he leave himself open to being preached at? Mr. Theodore had always had an eclectic spiritual bent. He sang in his church choir, he was at ease discussing the Dalai Lama over the back fence. He usually had a book in hand of philosophy or poetry: Leopold, Thoreau, Frost.

But in his more honest moments, Michael wondered if maybe he'd actually said yes *hoping* his aging, well-read neighbor had an answer to the bankruptcy of his own spirit.

Everybody else seemed to have answers, theories about life and death and meaning, that they were, in Michael's opinion, much too eager to share.

Mr. Theodore, however, had given no advice. While Michael rebuilt front steps and installed new windows, Mr. Theodore offered only small talk—how to look after geraniums, which of the neighbors made the best chocolate chip cookies—and endless work. When one job ended at his aging house another magically appeared.

But six in the morning? Mr. Theodore was pressing his luck. "I was just wondering—"

Michael sighed inwardly, tried to guess. What hadn't he seen? What repair had he overlooked in Mr. Theodore's project-ridden house? Leaking roof? Dripping bathroom sink? Despite the hour, and a monstrous hangover, Michael was aware of feeling relieved. Something to do today, after all.

There was always something else to do, thank God. With nothing to do, Michael would surely be more lost than he already was, as lost as he had been before Mr. Theodore had come and knocked on his door for the first time and pulled him away from the perfect digital images of the huge plasma television set, the only purchase he had made with all that money.

Michael Brewster had not expected to end up unspeakably, unbelievably rich, at twenty-seven years of age. Had he ever dreamed it, he surely would not have seen it as a curse. But it was. And he would give all that money back in an instant if only—

"Christmas lights," Mr. Theodore announced happily.

He must have registered Michael's confused look.

"Christmas," Mr. Theodore said. "It's almost Christmas. Today is—" he consulted his watch for confirmation "—November 15. I always put up my decorations on November 15."

But Michael hadn't gotten much past the Christmas part. Peripherally, on the edges of the haze he lived in, he must have realized stores were decorating for Christmas, that fall color was gone and winter-gray had set in.

And yet, it felt as if he'd had no warning. Michael was swamped with feeling. Christmas? Already? How? For a shocking moment he could smell the tang of pine, and his mother's pies baking, his father's aftershave. He could hear his brother's laughter, the ripping of tissue…the sensation of loss and of loneliness nearly knocked him off his feet.

And the question that burned in him, that made him toss and turn at night, that made him pace the floor, that made him drink too much beer and stare for hours at a TV screen in an effort to shut it out, was suddenly right there on his tongue. He tried to bite it back but it felt as though the question was going to strangle him if he did not ask someone, say the words, finally, out loud.

"How will I survive?" Michael Brewster said. His voice seemed normal enough, but an icy wind picked that moment to howl, and to turn his voice into a desperate whisper.

It was as he thought, as he dreaded: there was no answer to that question.

Still, Mr. Theodore touched his arm, and he found himself looking into eyes that were blue and ageless and full of strength and compassion.

"Find someone in more pain than you," the old man said firmly, "and help them."

Michael expelled his breath. An impossible solution. No one was in more pain than him. No one.

He said gruffly, "Where do you keep your Christmas lights?"

As it turned out, Mr. Theodore kept his Christmas lights in his garage. As it turned out, he kept enough outdoor Christmas decorations to rival Santa Claus. There were strings and strings and strings of house lights, acorn wreaths for the windows and doors, an electric waving Santa and a complete set of reindeer for the roof. There were life-size models of Mary and Joseph, a lean-to stable to house them and a donkey, for the front yard.

Michael was wrestling with that two-hundred-pound donkey when Mr. Theodore appeared and handed him a neatly folded piece of paper.

"What we talked about earlier," he said. He gave the plywood donkey a happy pat, as if the damned creature lived, which Michael had been beginning to suspect. Then Mr. Theodore shivered, looked at Michael's bare arms, shook his head and disappeared back inside his house.

What had they talked about earlier?

With the first snow of the year falling, imperious to the Michigan wind most people would have found impossibly bitter, Michael glared at the paper. He needed a lifeline, not a quote from the Bible, or the Dalai Lama or Thoreau or whoever Mr. Theodore was currently fascinated with. Still, he curbed the desire to crumple the paper and throw it away unread. Mr. Theodore, after all, had not given him poetry, or Bible verses or Thoreau so far. Maybe there was something on this paper he could hold on to. He opened it with the rough impatience of a man afraid to hope.

What was written there was a scrawled address at the east end of Washington Avenue. Michael recognized it as being in the rough part of Treemont, down by the old abandoned flour mill. Underneath the address was written a name.

Michael remembered their conversation from earlier. *Find someone in more pain than you and help them.*

As if, he thought cynically.

Still, the words printed untidily on the paper intrigued him. Pulled at him. The words said *The Secret Santa Society.*

Thirty-nine days until Christmas…

"I need an elf," Kirsten Morrison said into the phone, "and not the one you sent me last year. I shouldn't be fussy about a free elf? He got drunk and fell off the sleigh."

A shiver went up and down her spine, she told herself only because the front door had opened, letting that chill breath of November in.

"A shortage of elves? Oh, a shortage of *volunteer* elves. So, what would I have to pay for an elf who wouldn't get drunk and fall off the sleigh?" She said it as if she had money to spare for an elf, which she didn't.

"Five hundred dollars? Are you kidding me? That's robbery! What kind of person would rob Santa?"

She peered out her office door to see who had come in. There was no clear line of vision anymore. Once a small market, the front part of her space was now crammed with toys. Sixteen tricycle boxes had arrived this afternoon and were practically blocking the front door.

Trikes that had to be assembled at some point, she made a quick mental note. That was still far down the priority list. She caught sight of her visitor and involuntarily drew in her breath, suddenly not sure it was the air that had chilled her.

He was a big man, maybe a hair under six feet, but with astounding breadth across the shoulders that he brushed snow from. He wore no gloves though winter had decided to arrive last night with a vengeance, and even peering past obstacles she noticed his hands.

Strong hands, capable hands. Hands that could make a woman aware that she was alone, and that there were things, no matter how fiercely independent she became, that she was just never going to be able to do.

He was that kind of man, all right. The kind of man who made a woman suddenly and acutely aware of yearnings she could manage to keep secret—even from herself—most of the time.

He was the beginning of a story that ended *happily ever after.* Gorgeous in a dark way: unruly hair the color of rich chocolate fell past his collar; whiskers roughened chiseled cheekbones, highlighted a chin carved by the gods, and framed a mouth with lips that were full and sensuous but unsmiling.

And his eyes! Lord have mercy!

They were a shade of green she had never seen before, somewhere between jade and emerald, and they were fringed with a sinfully sooty abundance of lashes.

"Be there in a sec," she called.

She turned from him, trying to focus on the business at hand. "Five hundred dollars for an elf! Where is your Christmas spirit? Oh! Same to you!"

She smashed down the phone, glared at it, but she was aware she was marshaling herself. Finally, she wove her way through the impromptu storage area the storefront had become. It was getting tight, and a few boxed dolls fell from the top of the last stack of toys she had to negotiate past before she could get to the tiny remaining space by the front door. Space filled by him.

He caught the toppling dolls before they hit the floor, moving with the smooth and effortless speed and grace of an athlete. It put him much too close to her, and she found herself having to crane her neck to look at him, at the same time as being enveloped by an aroma that was clean and crisp and utterly, intoxicatingly male.

Shoot, if he wasn't even more compelling to look at close up than he had been from a distance! Except for his eyes. This close to him, Kirsten could see something shadowed the green, like ice forming on a forest pond. She tried to name that *something* and failed. Whatever it was, it put the chill that had swept in the door with him to shame.

He looked at the dolls, both dressed in extravagant princess frills, and handed them to her as if they might burn his hand if he held them too long.

"Thanks," she said drily. She refrained from adding, *As far as I know these dolls do not come in a model that bites big, masculine guys.* Mores the pity, she decided.

"Somehow, you don't look like you're here to deliver a Santa list," she said, when he didn't volunteer what had brought him inside the door clearly marked The Secret Santa Society.

He didn't reply. In fact, he reached behind him and shut the door, which was leaking cold air, with a snap.

"Oh." Kirsten had been warned it was a rough part of town. She'd been told over and over to lock the door when she was in the building by herself. But what if someone came to deliver a list and the door was locked? Even one mom, turned away…she shivered.

Besides, the awareness she felt for this man that had appeared in her space was not of the fearful variety though certainly of the *dangerous* variety.

He was a man attractive enough to make a girl who had given up on fairy tales feel strangely threatened, as if a review of her belief system might be in order. It had been four years, after all…

"So, no Santa list," she said, aware her cheer was forced, that she was fighting something within herself, "What can I do for you?"

He was watching her with the faintest interest touching his eyes, eyes that seemed deeper and darker the longer she looked at him, but no warmer. There was something in them that reminded her of an iceberg—magnificently beautiful, but fearsome and remote, untouchable.

"I heard you were looking for an elf."

She was not sure she would have been more shocked if he said he was looking for The Treemont School of Ballet. The words, faintly playful, did not match his eyes. His delivery was absolutely deadpan, and then she realized he had overheard her conversation. She waited for him to smile—to see if a smile would warm his gaze—but no smile was forthcoming. It was as if he could say the words that were tinged with humor—since he was obviously the man least likely to ever be mistaken for an elf—but somehow they couldn't break through the ice that shrouded his eyes.

"Ah," she said. "An elf. I'm in desperate need of one, but I'm afraid you're the wrong size. No applicants over four foot eleven. Last year's was four foot seven."

She found herself holding her breath waiting to see if he would smile.

"But he got drunk." He'd heard a lot of that conversation. Still no smile. Anyone who was not going to smile over a four-foot-seven drunken elf probably wasn't going to smile about anything. It had the ridiculous effect of making her feel as if she *had* to make him smile, even though she was more than aware her belief system was on shaky ground, and she

shouldn't be testing its strength.

"He got very rude," she said, ignoring the *shouldn't*. "He kept asking Santa to pull his finger." In her eagerness to make him smile, she could feel that telltale hint of heat in her chest.

As a schoolgirl, Kirsten had been tormented by blushing. In more recent years, she'd been able to head off the embarrassing tide of crimson by thinking, quickly, of something—anything—else. For some reason the fish display at

O'Malley's Market provided some of the most powerful mind-diverting pictures. Trout, eye in.

"Sounds like a good reason to trade in for bigger elves," he said. "Those small ones can be so unpredictable."

"We've never had a large elf!" Rules. She found refuge in rules.

"Sorry to hear that—it's probably an unfair hiring practice, punishable under the equal opportunities act."

"Actually, I think it's impersonating an elf that is punishable by something." For some horrible reason the word *spanking* came to mind and for a minute she had to close her eyes and picture freshly filleted perch. When she opened them, she said, more weakly than she intended, "Forced ingestion of Christmas cake, egg nog and Christmas carols!"

Still no smile, but just a hint of something in those mysterious eyes, the tiniest spark of sunlight flashing across green ice.

"Now who is impersonating whom?" he asked. "I heard you claim on the phone you were Santa. An obvious lie. Santa would never think of cake, egg nog and carols as a punishment. Plus, no white beard, no belly like jelly."

She was the one who smiled then, reluctantly delighted by this spontaneous, *dangerous* exchange with a most mysterious stranger on a dull, gray afternoon. She smiled until the exact moment she became aware, and acutely so, that he was inspecting her!

She realized she looked about as far from the heroine of a *happily ever after* kind of story as anyone could look. The warehouse section of the building, behind her office, could get cold and very dusty. She was wearing a faded brown skirt, warm tights, sensible shoes, a cardigan worn at the elbows. Her hair suddenly seemed horrible, and she wished she would have let Lulu, one of the volunteers, streak the mousy-brown to blond last week when the woman had practically begged her to let her do it.

"Kirstie" Lulu had said. "You're twenty-three. You shouldn't look forty!"

Naturally, now she wondered if she looked forty today! That, she told herself, was what a man did.

All of a sudden, a woman who had not been on a serious date in four years *on purpose* was worried about her cardigan and her hair color and was thinking, wistfully, of the donation of twenty-four shades of lipstick sitting, unopened, on her desk.

All of a sudden a woman who was pragmatic to a fault was thinking *if Cinderella can do it, so can I.*

"I can't help it if your vision of Santa is limited," she said, trying valiantly not to show how flustered her own treacherous thoughts were making her. "Around here, I am Santa. Or at least the spirit of Santa. I make sure the kids in this neighborhood get Christmas gifts."

"Even the most liberal of them must be shocked to find out *you're* Santa," he said.

He did not seem moved by her altruism. If anything, a cynical line deepened around his mouth. It annoyed Kirsten to realize that she wanted him, a complete stranger, to be impressed with her activities and accomplishments, probably because she knew her appearance had failed to impress him in any way.

"Well, they don't find out. That's why it's the *Secret* Santa Society. We elect one of the volunteers to play Santa. The election is the highlight of our volunteer party." Now she was giving him all kinds of dull information he couldn't possibly want, and she was aware she felt aggravated and defensive.

Why? Because of the cynical downturn of his mouth? Because he was looking at her like she was a Goody Two-shoes?

Because she could have had her hair streaked and hadn't?

It was time, obviously, to end this encounter.

"So, unless you're going to sue me because I have no elf positions available, I have a lot of work to do."

When was the last time she'd been this rattled by a guy?

That was easy. Her one and only serious relationship, her first year of college. James Moriarty. He'd pretended he liked her—no, was *smitten* with her—for a heady six weeks or so. He had really wanted help cheating on his math exam.

And then there was Kent, her brother-in-law—ex-brother-in-law—*pretending* to be Mr. Boy-Next-Door, the perfect husband. But when the whole family had most needed him to be strong, what had he been doing? Playing footsie—and much more—with his secretary.

She shivered. And that was why she was sworn off fairy tales. Men, in all their thousands of guises, were never what they wanted you to think they were. Especially fickle would-be ones like this one: big, athletic, sure of himself, drop-dead gorgeous.

Though this man in front of her did seem to be without pretense, something so real lurking in the depths of those astonishing cold, hot eyes that it threatened her heart's armor. She tried to put her finger on it. *Lost?* No, not quite, though the very thought added an intriguing layer to the man who stood there dripping confidence and melting snow.

Predictably, he ignored her dismissal, "Even I'm not hardhearted enough to sue the Secret Santa Society."

Confirming what she already could see in the cast of his face. He was world-weary in some way. Cynical.

Not the jovial grandfatherly type who usually stopped by to volunteer.

"So, no available elf position," she said. She fully intended for it to sound like a breezy dismissal, but even she could hear the renegade regret in her voice as if she truly would like to give him a position even though a man like him would never really volunteer at an organization like this, and even though she had decided she didn't like him. Or at least didn't like what he was doing to her. Then she blushed.

It came without the warning heat in her chest first, no time to ward it off with visual images of fresh fillets. When she blushed, her whole face went crimson, from jawline to forehead, like a red Christmas light blinking to life.

And then he did smile, finally, just a tease of one, a slight curl of lip, as if smiling might hurt him. The smile didn't have a hope of touching what was in those eyes.

"I can do other things," he said. "Besides be an elf."

"Like what?" she gasped. Ridiculous to ask. He had said it reluctantly and she had already decided she wanted him out of here. He was the kind of man who could hurt a woman—especially one like her—very badly. He could do it without half trying, and he could do it without looking back.

The smile was gone completely. He regarded her thoughtfully for a long moment. The moment stretched.

She realized, wildly, that she had left herself wide-open. Of course there were other things he could do and do well. The shape of his lips, for instance, suggested he would be an amazing kisser. All kinds of men would have jumped on the opportunity to let her know that, and all the other skills that she was missing out on, too.

But this man did not take the opportunity, thankfully, to flirt with her, even though he looked like a man who would be very comfortable flirting with women. Gorgeous women, who streaked their hair and managed to get some lipstick on every day, and wore hip-hugging tight jeans instead of frumpy brown skirts.

Kirsten's flirting days, if they could be called that, were far, far behind her. And somehow, maybe because of that secret his eyes were trying to tell her, she suspected his were, too.

She thought he was not going to answer at all, And then he said, gruffly, reluctantly, "I guess that depends. Is there anything else you need done?"

Her thoughts were renegade. What woman could be in a room with a man like this and not think of all the things a woman alone would like done?

That little knot rubbed out of the tender place where her shoulder joined her neck, for starters.

She was stunned at herself.

Four years. Virtually a nun. Wanting it that way. The breakup of her sister Becky's marriage—a love Kirsten had unabashedly idolized—had broken something in Kirsten, too. Becky and Kent had begun dating just after the James fiasco, and just as Kirsten's own parents were ending their twenty-year union. Still a teenager, impressionable, hopeful, naive, Kirsten had transferred her need to *believe* in love—in forever—to Becky and Kent. Instead, in the end, they had reinforced her deepest fear: things that seemed strong could be so, so heartbreakingly fragile.

"Is that why you're here?" she said, not trying to hide her incredulity. "To volunteer?"

He hesitated, nodded. Sort of nodded, the slightest inclination of his head. "I'm a carpenter by trade. Anything you need built?"

She sighed. Even if she took his offer more practically, there was so much she needed done. Sixteen tricycles to begin with. Of course he wasn't really here to help her, though there was nothing she could use right now like a strong, healthy man to unload trucks, to put heavy items up on high shelves. And a carpenter? Every year they built a sleigh to deliver gifts. It was built on top of the rickety flat-deck trailer in the warehouse. Every year she was amazed someone didn't get hurt, and that it didn't rattle apart.

But to invite a temptation like him into her space? This was her world. It was where everything was in her control—and she wasn't surrendering that for a better sleigh!

Besides, she found it hard to believe he'd come here to volunteer. He just wasn't the type. No, he'd taken a wrong turn somewhere, and decided to amuse himself at her expense for a few moments.

In a fairy-tale world, he would be the answer to unassembled trikes and a safe sleigh for Santa. In a fairy-tale world he would be the answer to everything including the fact that sometimes in the night she awoke and felt almost weak with loneliness.

But she had learned the brutally hard way there were no fairy tales, and a woman was wise to be totally independent, to rely only on herself.

She folded her arms firmly over her chest.

What was it, lingering just beneath that ice in his eyes, that made her think something else was there? Something that you could trust with your secret burdens?

Something that would break your heart in two more likely, she warned herself.

As if her heart wasn't already broken in two. Hers. Her

sister's. Her brother-in-law's. Her nephew's. A world that had seemed so strong, a vow that had seemed unbreakable, gone in one second.

She turned back toward her office, remembering the relative safety of all her pressures, not wanting to dwell on things broken, a category this man seemed like he might fit in. She had no time for an encounter like this one, nor was she brave enough to find out exactly what his offhanded offer might mean.

"I have to find an elf," she said, dismissing him, yet again. "And fifty kids' winter jackets would be nice. That's what I need done."

There. That should be enough to scare him off.

Then again, he did not have the look of a man easily scared. Silence. She glanced back at him. He had not moved, there was a little puddle on the floor where the snow was melting off of him. He was wearing a black leather jacket, worn, and not warm enough for today, and jeans with a hole clear through the knee, not a day to be showing bare skin, either.

Rather than making him look poor, the old jacket and the worn jeans had a certain cachet.

She realized she was looking at a man who didn't care— not about what he looked like, not about the cold, maybe not about anything at all.

He was exactly the kind of man her mother had always warned her about. But then that was one of the illusions she'd had to leave behind. That her mother knew best.

Her mother, who couldn't glue her own marriage back together, her mother who had approved of Kent for Becky… Kirsten shook her head, looked away from him, troubled, looked back in time to see him nod, once, curtly. He turned and disappeared back out the door, leaving another frosty wave in his wake.

She was aware of craning her neck to see where he went, but the snow was still coming down hard, and he disappeared into it with a phantomlike quality, as if maybe he had never been in the first place.

She frowned. She wasn't quite sure what had happened there.

"Strange encounter of the weird kind," she said, shrugging it off and moving back to her office. She looked at her calendar. Thirty-nine days!

Way, way too much to be done, and not nearly enough time left to do it. She had not one second to spare on thinking about green eyes like those ones. What was in them? *Loneliness*. No. *Aloneness*.

Closer. The aloneness of a man who had seen hell, she decided. To feel sympathy for him, to be drawn toward the mystery in those eyes would be the most dangerous thing of all.

Not one second, she chided herself. The door opened again, and she whirled back, disgusted that she wanted it to be him.

But it wasn't. It was Mr. Temple, the neighborhood postman, only these days he wasn't just delivering her mail.

"Those Johansson kids are poor. They don't expect nothin', they don't even hope. Imagine those poor little mites not hopin' for anything. I told them to just pretend it could happen."

"And?" she said.

He passed her a note, a glisten in his eyes, her most enthusiastic researcher, neighborhood spy and conspirator.

It had the boys' address on it, she recognized it as a particularly dilapidated apartment on Fifth Street. Hans wanted a bike. Lars wanted a basketball.

"Got it," she said, and for a moment she felt the weight of

these new wishes that had been entrusted to her. It didn't matter that there wasn't enough money or time. Every year it seemed she would run out of both, and every year miracles happened. A few more phone calls, a few more letters, a few more radio shows. Besides, it was always a relief to get requests that could be fulfilled. She had a file—the Impossible Dreams File—of ones that could not.

"I've got something else for you, Kirstie." He held it out with pleasure.

She couldn't believe it. "Where on earth did you get this?" she asked, taking the catalog reverently from him.

"I'd tell you," he kidded, "but then I'd have to kill you."

It was the *Little in Love* Special Christmas Catalog. Only those who had reached the tier of Serious Collector of the precious figurines received it, and Kirsten was fairly sure she would never be one of those. Currently she ranked on Tier One, a Little Fan. On the tiny salary she was paid here, she could manage only one new figurine a year. Including gifts, and the odd find at a secondhand store, Kirsten now owned twelve of the hundreds of figurines that were available.

Little in Love was a collection of hand-painted porcelain bisque figurines that artist Lou Little had created in the 1950s. All the figurines were of a young couple, Harriet and Smedley, and depicted delightful scenes of their love. Little had captured something that captured hearts: innocence, wonder, delight in each other, and he never seemed to run out of material.

Trying not to appear too eager or too rude, Kirsten scurried back to her office and shut the door. She opened the catalog with tender fingers and gasped.

In an astonishing departure from tradition, the new Christmas collectibles were called *A Little History* and showed Harriet and Smedley in different times in history: here he was a World War I flying ace, leaning out of his plane to kiss Harriet goodbye, here he was as a pioneer building a Little house, Harriet looking on.

Then she saw it. *A Knight in Shining Armor.* She thought it was the most beautiful Little piece she had ever seen with Smedley, visor up, astride a magnificent white horse, leaning down to kiss Harriet's hand.

She looked at the price, winced and mentally filed the piece—everything in this catalog—in her own impossible dreams file. Reluctantly, she put the catalog away. She would take it home with her and pore over the pictures later.

Really, the catalog should have been more than enough to sweep that other encounter right from her mind. So she was amazed, and annoyed, that it had not. Her mind kept wandering from the bookkeeping tasks. Not that engrossing, but as the Secret Santa Society's founder and only paid employee, one of her biggest responsibilities. Rather than Smedley on horseback proving a distraction to her afternoon, it was eyes as coolly green as pond ice that she kept thinking of.

"And that is why you don't even deserve to be a Serious Collector," she reprimanded herself firmly.

CHAPTER TWO

WHEN Michael Brewster headed back out the door of The Secret Santa Society it was snowing harder. The office was on the mean end of Washington, most of the storefronts boarded up, shadows in the doorways. He noticed a man huddled in the doorway next to her building. Waiting for an opportunity to slip through that door and help himself?

She had paper taped over her own windows, probably to keep kids from peeking in at all her top-secret activities, but from a security point of view it would have been better if she left the windows unblocked.

Michael gave the man a look that sent him scuttling.

It was not the kind of neighborhood where a woman should be working alone—especially not with every available space in the made-over store stuffed with, well, stuff. Teddy bears, MP3 players, trikes, dolls in cellophane wrappers, including those embarrassing two that had fallen into his hands.

She was the kind of woman who made a guy feel protective. Maybe it was because her clothes had been baggy, that she had seemed tiny and fragile. Still, even with the lumpiness of the dress, she hadn't been able to totally disguise slender curves, a lovely femininity that might make her very vulnerable at this desperate end of Washington. And it wasn't as if she would have the physical strength to protect herself. Her wrists had been so tiny he had actually wanted to circle them between his thumb and pointer finger to see if they were as impossibly small as they looked.

And those eyes! Intensely gray, huge, fringed with the most astonishing display of natural lash he had ever seen. Her eyes had saved her from plainness.

Something about her reluctantly intrigued him—maybe the fact that she so underplayed her every asset.

What was she thinking, being alone with all that stuff in this neighborhood? Was she impossibly brave or simply stupid? Still, you had to give it to someone who was shopping around for an elf. There were probably special angels who looked after people like that.

He frowned at the thought, renegade and unwanted. He, of all people, knew there were no special angels, not for anyone. So he had obeyed Mr. Theodore. He'd come to this address thinking he was going to find someone in worse shape than him.

It obviously had not been her.

She had not been beautiful, not even pretty, really, unless he counted her eyes. He thought of them again—luminescent, brimming with a light that could almost make a man forget she was wearing a sweater just like the ones his granny used to knit. Her hair had struck him as hopelessly old-fashioned, but for some reason he'd liked it. It was just plain light brown, falling in a wave past her shoulder, no particular style.

She was one of those kind of girls he remembered only

vaguely from high school—bookwormish, smart, capable…
and invisible. She was not the kind who pretended fear of
spiders or dropped her books coquettishly when a male of
interest was in the vicinity. She did not color her hair blond
or paint her lips red or have fingernails that left marks on a
man's back, her lashes would not melt when she cried.

In other words, she was not the kind of woman he knew
the first thing about.

Nor did he want to, though that fleeting thought of *her* fingernails and *his* back made him shiver, which was startling.
He had not reacted to a woman in a very long time. He had
probably *never* reacted to a woman who was anything like her:
understated, intelligent, *pure*.

Women, he reminded himself, took energy. He had none.
It was that simple.

And a woman like that one manning the Secret Santa
Society office would take more energy than most because
despite her plainness, those multifaceted eyes made him
suspect a very complicated nature. *Deep. Sensitive.
Intelligent. Funny.*

It annoyed him that he was even thinking of her. His assignment, if he could call it that, was to find someone in
worse pain than himself.

Not Ms. Secret Santa, obviously, hunting for elves and
brimming with faith that her good deeds alone could protect
her from this neighborhood.

But there were kids out there who needed jackets, and the
first true cold snap of the year had arrived. He wondered what
kind of pain it caused a parent who was not to be able to buy
a jacket for a child who was cold.

Not worse pain than his own, *different* pain than his own.

Maybe that was why Mr. Theodore had sent him, knowing there would be something here to keep him distracted as Christmas approached. Christmas, a time of family. A time of pain for families who had nothing.

And for a guy who had nothing instead of a family.

He drew his breath in sharply, forced himself to focus. It was one day at a time, one step at a time, one task at a time. Right now, his task was fifty jackets and an elf. Michael shook his head like a boxer who had been sucker punched.

It seemed like the most unlikely lifeline, but it was the only one he was being offered, and if he didn't find something to give a damn about, and soon, that question was going to burn a little deeper into him.

How will I survive?

His world gone. Nothing left of it. The snow swirled around him, and he realized he should be cold, but he didn't get cold anymore. Twice a year, he'd given up carpentry. The whole family put their lives on hold and headed to Alaska for the crab fishery.

After surviving six hours in the icy, gray waters of the Bering Sea, Michael did not get cold anymore. Or really ever warm, either. He was stuck in a place where it was neither hot nor cold. Purely a place of survival.

He focused on the task at hand, just as at Mr. Theodore's house he focused only on what was in front of him: broken stairs, a rotten window casing, a leaky faucet. There were many ways to shut off the human mind. He stopped at the nearest phone booth. Most of the telephone book was gone, but his righteousness was being rewarded today. The clothing section of the yellow pages was intact.

But then he realized he wasn't quite sure what he wanted.

Big coats or small coats? Boys or girls? What about babies? Styles? Sizes?

He glanced back down the street. He could go ask her *exactly* what she wanted, but he didn't want to. He found himself wanting to surprise her, because it had been clear from the look on her face she had no expectations of him at all. She didn't even think he'd be back. Maybe didn't even *want* him to come back, which was not the normal reaction he got from women.

And he still had that option, of not going back, of leaving that strangely engaging encounter one hundred percent behind him. Looking at coats some little kids *needed* might make him feel something, in fact he felt jumpy thinking about it. How could he do an assignment like this and not be touched in some way? It was a fact the crafty Mr. Theodore had probably already considered!

Didn't Mr. Theodore know that if the dam inside of Michael ever broke open, the torrent would be dangerous and destructive, wrecking everything in its path?

No. He could not go shopping for coats. But, on the other hand, fifty kids without coats? He swore under his breath, and the word came out in a frosty puff that reminded him how cold it was getting. Michael realized he could not *not* go shopping for coats.

He said the word again, and realized it was not an appropriate word for an emissary of the Secret Santa Society, not even an unofficial one.

Michael looked again at the pretty much demolished phone book and guiltily tore out one of the few remaining pages, the one that listed coats on it. And then he tore out the preceding one, as well, the one that listed clowns. Clowns were related to elves, weren't they?

Guilt, he thought with surprise. That was a feeling of sorts, the first one he'd had in a long time.

Unless he could count what he felt talking to Ms. Santa back there.

Not actual warmth, but a remembrance of warmth. A remembrance of what it was to *want* something. What had he wanted? He frowned. To connect with her. To share a little normal, everyday banter with another human being. He'd liked making her blush. It had been amusing.

It had been a long, long time since he had felt even the smallest shiver of interest in anything or anyone. So here he was less than an hour into his mysterious assignment, and having feelings sneak up on him.

But was it going to be enough to save him? Or would it destroy what was left of him? He decided to have a little tiny bit of faith, and realized with a sigh that was another concept that had been foreign to his world for a long, long time.

Well, he thought, if a man starts messing with the spirit of Santa, some surprising things were going to happen. That was a given.

He found the address he had ripped out of the phone book. It was in a different world than the office of the Secret Santa Society, part of a brightly lit strip mall that housed upscale factory outlets on the edge of a neighborhood where the houses started in the half-million-dollar range. The Christmas displays were up in the windows, and lights blinked cheer against the colorlessness of the day.

He entered a store called West Coats. More Christmas: a tree decorated totally in white, updated versions of carols blaring from a public address system. He hated this.

Then he was nearly bowled over by a salesclerk who was

exactly his type. Blond, tall, willowy, her lipstick a perfect match for her fingernails, a red Santa hat at a jaunty angle on her head. Her tag said her name was Calypso.

The woman at the Secret Santa Society had not been wearing a name tag. He realized he had not asked her name. He bet it would be a good, sturdy, practical name like Helen or Susan or Gwen.

"I need fifty kids' coats," he told Calypso, who leaned way toward him and gave him a look at the top of her lacy bra. Red, to match her hat. The surprising thing happened: not one vision of *her* fingernails and *his* back, no matter how hard he tried to conjure it.

"Fifty coats!" She giggled and blinked her heavily made-up lashes. Considering how he was freshly aware of wanting to *connect*, he was now aware of not wanting to connect with her in more than a businesslike way.

Somehow, painfully, he managed to pick out fifty children's coats. He wanted practical coats that would keep them warm and survive snowball fights and the making of forts and snow angels. He picked out coats in as many different sizes and colors as he could find. He tossed onto his growing stack a few little sleeping bags with hoods, which Calypso cooed over and called bunting bags.

And at the last minute, hesitating, he chose three little pink princess jackets with fur collars and cuffs on them. They felt in his hands the same way those dolls had—foreign, fragile, too delicate. He knew they were totally impractical. And yet he could not put them back.

"There," he said, "Done."

"What do you want all these coats for?" Calypso asked.

He was afraid if he explained his mission it would just bring more cooing, so he only shrugged.

"I can get you a discount if it's for a charity," she said.

"No, it's okay." He was aware as he passed her his credit card that this was the first time he had enjoyed one single cent of all that money, huge state-of-the-art plasma television set included.

She insisted on helping him carry the coats out to his car, even though he tried to discourage her.

"Oh," she breathed when she saw the car. "A Jaguar."

He saw his appeal to her had just intensified. Once upon a time, he would have played that for all it was worth. He had a sharp memory of all the times he and Brian had cruised in this car…

"It's my brother's car," he said abruptly.

With his car so stuffed with coats he could no longer see out his back window, he was aware Calypso was still standing there, hugging herself against the cold. All those coats and she hadn't put one on?

She was waiting for something, so he said, "I don't suppose you'd know where I can find an elf?"

She popped her gum and settled a hand on a cocked hip. "Ooh," she said playfully, "I wouldn't have figured you for kinky."

For some reason he thought of another woman. And her blush. A woman who probably wouldn't use the word kinky with a man even if she'd known him for fifty years, never mind for a little over an hour. A woman who probably wouldn't know the difference between a Jaguar and a Honda Civic.

A red fingernailed hand—an exact match for the hat and bra—was laid on his jacket sleeve.

"I'm available for dinner," Calypso announced, her voice sultry and her made-up eyes inviting.

She was exactly the kind of woman he'd always gone for. A girl who knew how to have a good time and who knew exactly how the game was played. If he was really going to start *connecting* again, if he was really ready, Calypso would be a safe way to do it.

Again, he thought of another woman. One who wouldn't have announced she was available for dinner if she'd gone four days without food.

And suddenly he found himself wondering if she was.

He wanted to find out if her name was Anne or Mary or Rose. Surely, for fifty jackets, she'd surrender her name. He couldn't wait to see her face when she saw the pink ones with the silly collars.

"Thanks for all your help. Sorry, no, I'm not available for dinner."

"How about your brother?" she said, running a covetous finger over the sleek blackness of the hood detail.

He did not risk evoking her sympathy by telling her his brother was dead. He forced a smile, but he felt like a wolf, baring its teeth in warning. "He isn't available, either."

She took it in stride, a woman who knew men were just like buses—another one would be along in a few minutes—winked at him and walked away putting lots of *swish* in it.

Michael put the car in gear and started driving back across town. Rush hour had begun with a vengeance, the still thickly falling snow not helping. He found himself in a tangle of cars on West Washington, glaring at his watch, thinking, *She'll have gone home by the time I get there.*

The traffic finally started moving, inching along through

the streets made treacherous with melting snow. He reached for the heater, turned it up a notch.

And then his hand fell away, and he contemplated what he had just done. Why had he turned up the heat? The windshield was clearly defrosting adequately.

When he focused, sure enough, there it was. The tiniest shiver along his spine. He realized he was feeling something. Cold. He felt just a tiny bit cold. He'd been getting warnings all afternoon that something was in movement. The guilt over tearing the pages from the telephone book. *Enjoying* spending the money on the coats. The desire to connect with *her*. Now this.

The shiver was already gone, and he deliberately turned the heat back down. He wasn't ready to feel anything. He certainly wasn't ready to go invite some woman he barely knew— he didn't even know her name, for God's sake—to have dinner with him.

He could send the coats to the Secret Santa Society by courier tomorrow. He could find her a damned elf without ever seeing her again, without immersing himself any further in this dangerous world that would make him *feel*.

He slammed on the brakes, slid, used the power of the slide to yank on the wheel and do a complete U-turn, dramatic, worthy of Hollywood. Horns honked their outrage. He didn't care. He was heading away from the Secret Santa Society as fast as he could!

Because his side and rear windows were nearly completely blocked with children's coats, he heard the siren before he saw the lights. Michael looked in his side mirror and sighed. The red and blue lights were flashing right behind him, and when he pulled over, the police car did, too.

The cop was not in the Christmas spirit. "That turn back

there was illegal—even if you could see, which you can't."
Out came the ticket book. And then he looked more closely
at Michael's cargo.

"What is this? You rob a store?"

It would be so easy to say yes, and see where that led.

"You got a receipt for this stuff?"

Michael passed him the receipt.

"Okay, so you *bought* fifty kids' coats. What's up with that?"

The cop didn't look like he was in the mood for the *none-
of-your-business* that Michael wanted to give him. In fact, the
man was trying very hard not to look as cold and miserable
as he obviously was.

Suddenly it seemed like it was the right thing to do to let
him know good happened in the world, too. It wasn't all
drunks hitting their wives and kids, dope dealers on the
corners, asses doing U-turns.

"The coats are for the Secret Santa Society." Michael
offered it up reluctantly, the man who least wanted to be seen
as a do-gooder.

The ticket book was snapped shut and replaced in its upper
pocket home, beside a name tag, Adams.

"You were delivering them?"

It seemed hopelessly complicated to say he had been delivering them, *then* decided not to deliver them, at least not
personally, so Michael only nodded.

The policeman looked at the clogged road. "Washington's
always like this at this time of day. Were you going to try
Wilmore instead?"

Michael decided for honesty. "Actually I was thinking
maybe I'd just go home, make the delivery a different day."

Adams frowned at the traffic, then brightened. "Emergency

delivery to the Secret Santa Society. Follow me," he ordered. His whole face and body language changed. He was *thrilled* to be part of something good.

So, that's what happened, Michael thought, when you fooled with something as powerful as Santa. He was now headed, under police escort, directly toward a place that moments ago he had decided he was not going. He pondered, uneasily, how much of his life was now going to be out of his control.

Then he reminded himself that thinking life was in your control was the largest of illusions anyway.

Sirens were nothing unusual for this neighborhood, in fact they played in the background, a noise Kirsten blocked out as easily as elevator music. There had been a rush of volunteers earlier, but they had all left at suppertime and now she was alone. Happily she pulled her catalog closer. *Love in a Little House on the Prairie*, was a wonderful piece, too. Not as good as *Knight in Shining Armor*, but—

The siren wailed, demanding attention, and suddenly the inside of her office was strobed in red and blue. Curious, she set aside the catalog and went to the front window. She peeled back a corner of the paper they used to keep curious kiddies from speculating what Santa might be up to this year.

A car, low slung, black and sexy—she thought it might be a Honda—was pulled over right in front of her office. To her practiced eye the car did not look like the more souped-up models the drug dealers favored.

And then the siren and lights were cut. The cop got out of his car and the driver got out of the sports car.

Him!

What was he doing back here? Uncharitably, Kirsten found herself hoping he was getting a ticket.

For being too good-looking and too sure of himself and for driving a car like that—a car that said he was sexy and sleek and way out of the league of a girl whose idea of excitement was poring over a catalog of porcelain figurines!

"You have to *want* to play to be in a league," she informed herself sternly. And she didn't. Okay, so she had moments of weakness, like this afternoon. That was only human. But generally she was extremely disciplined at keeping the larger picture in mind: love was fragile and easily breakable and not to be trusted.

She told herself to go back to her catalog—the only kind of love she planned to invest in. Instead, she found herself watching, unwittingly fascinated, as he walked back to the policeman with utter confidence. Even she, who had never been pulled over in her entire life, knew you were supposed to stay in your car. That rule surely applied doubly in this neighborhood. Having a gun pulled on him and being yelled at should take a bit of that masculine swagger out of his step!

But he didn't get a gun pulled on him, or get yelled at. No, he and the policeman seemed to be best of buddies. She sighed and realized even with his hands up and a gun pointed at him, he would have been the same. He was one of those most annoying men who carried something—some certainty— deep inside himself. It showed in the ease with which he was engaged in conversation with the policeman. Not intimidated. On firm footing, knowing himself to be equals with anyone.

The cop did appear to be writing him a ticket, which he took without glancing at, and put in the pocket of that same leather jacket. He didn't appear cold, though night was now falling and the temperature was dipping. The cop was shifting from foot to foot, and had his shoulders hunched against the cold.

The radio in the police car went off and the cop jogged back to his car. Moments later the siren was wailing and he was gone.

And *he* was leaning in the door of his car, filling his arms with…coats.

He staggered toward her door, and she had to run out in the snow and grab one of the jackets before it fell off the huge heap in his arms. The coat was pink, with fake fur trim, absolutely adorable, a coat a man like him could not possibly have chosen!

She raced back in ahead of him to clear a spot on a table.

"Set them here," she said breathlessly.

He set the coats down—at least twenty of them—and for a moment she simply stared. He had not brought her old secondhand junk, but brand-new winter jackets. From West Coats, no less, and in every shape and size and color. The price tags were still on them.

"I'll get the rest of them," he said.

"The rest of them?"

"You said fifty."

Some emotion clawed at her throat so big she thought it would choke her. Thankfully a flash to halibut worked on all kinds of feelings!

By the time he came back, and dumped another armload on the table, Kirsten was feeling quite composed, as if people delivered fifty brand-new West Coats jackets to her all the time. Unfortunately, on the very top was another pink jacket, trimmed at the collar and cuffs with fake fur, and she had to think of the sockeye salmon to get her feelings under control.

"Okay," she said, finally, folding her arms against the emotion she was still wrestling with, "who are you?"

He stuck out his hand. "Michael Brewster."

She took it and felt a shiver of awareness so strong it nearly took what was left of her breath away. She saved this one for moments just like this: the live lobster tank.

"Kirsten Morrison," she managed to stammer, visualizing like crazy.

"Kirsten," he repeated slowly. Was that surprise in his voice?

It seemed so unfair. How dare he be this good-looking, this self-assured, and kind, too? For a girl who worked with Santa, she was realistic to a fault about what life was really like. What *men* were really like. Treacherous, like James, or worse, like her brother-in-law, who had seemed like the boy next door. The man least likely to have an affair with his secretary.

Thankfully, when she looked in Michael's eyes, she was not sure it was kindness she saw. In fact, she was almost certain it was not. Sadness?

No, bigger than that. Something had happened to his soul.

"So, what did you get the ticket for?" she asked abruptly, trying to think of anything except his soul, and his lips and his hands and the way snow was melting in his thick dark hair.

"Ticket?" he looked puzzled. "Oh. It wasn't a ticket." He reached into his pocket. "A check. For the pink jacket. Or another one like it. Officer Adams insisted. I had him make it out to the Society."

Kirsten stared at him, took the check that he proffered.

"There's a phone number written on the back. His union or something. He said if you called, they'd probably make a donation."

It wasn't bad enough that he was so good-looking it hurt? He had to be a miracle worker, too? He could conjure jackets and checks out of thin air? If he really found an elf, then what?

There wouldn't be enough lobster tanks in the world to protect her! Her resolve was being tested, that's what.

No matter how many jackets he could find, this man in front of her was not a prince. Life was not a fairy tale. There was no happily-ever-after. Her parents had not made it, Becky and Kent had not made it, there were toads disguised as princes, like James Moriarty, everywhere.

"Why are you doing this?" she asked, aware she sounded far from grateful.

"You asked me to. Fifty coats. I haven't been able to locate an elf yet."

"Did they give them to you?"

"Give them to me? The coats?" he sounded genuinely baffled. "No."

"That's the *why*," she said tenaciously. "Why would you buy coats for a complete stranger?"

"Well, I didn't buy them for *you*," he said, which put her in her place, a warning that it was only a matter of time before a guy like this put a girl like her in her place. "I bought them for kids who need them."

She could see he simply didn't intend to tell her the *why* that she wanted to know, which was what had motivated this astonishing show of generosity.

"You're telling me *you* bought a coat that looked like this?" She glanced at the table, unfolded an arm to point at the princess jacket. "Three coats that look like this?"

He ducked his head, scratched the toe of his boot against the floor. "I was scraping the bottom of the barrel," he said gruffly. "That's all they had left when I reached forty-seven."

How could she know he was lying? She barely knew him! She didn't know him at all! She had no gift for telling when men were lying! She had believed in her brother-in-law long after her sister had given up. Didn't she still sometimes wish Kent would come through? Be the man she knew he was? Chase down her sister, beg her forgiveness? Hadn't she hoped, long after her parents' breakup, that it was all a mistake and they would be reunited?

She shook off the thought roughly, recognizing her weakness for fantasy. A man like the one in front of her did that. Made a woman long for tradition, stability, and for men who did not lie.

And yet she knew that was a lie about the coats. How could there be such a thing as a nice *lie?* And how could she fight the monster of tenderness that threatened to swamp her as she thought about this big, self-assured intensely masculine man buying such adorable coats for three little girls he had never met and probably never would meet?

She turned back to the jackets to hide the tears that stung at her eyes at the total collapse of her defenses. That was the problem when you pulled out the lobster tank too early in the game.

"Brand-new," she whispered. "Do you know how often these kids receive a brand-new jacket?" She caught sight of one of the price tags. The jacket was down-filled. That price times fifty?

So, she could add rich to his growing list of attractions. Except when she looked at him, she did not get the impression money gave him any joy. She did not get the impression anything gave him joy anymore.

A joyless liar. How could that possibly be so attractive?

"I don't know what to say," she stammered.

"How about that you'll go have dinner with me."

She shot him a look, looked away. It was obvious the invitation had taken him almost as much by surprise as it had her.

And she knew she couldn't go have dinner with him.

Because he was the kind of man a girl like her could fall for, and fall hard, and it was all downhill from there. She would build a fairy tale around him, he would wreck the ending.

There is no happily-ever-after, she told herself angrily. Still, saying no was about the hardest thing she'd ever done, because a little voice inside her was saying, *well, what about happy until?*

"Oh," she said, and each syllable was a torture. "I can't. Sorry. Not possibly." She waved vaguely at her stacks of toys. "Tricycles that need to be assembled." Just this morning that had been on the bottom of her priority list! How a man like him could change things!

She thought of the catalog in her office, how she should be longing to get back to Harriet and Smedley, and wasn't.

She glanced at him again and saw that she had astonished him. He was not accustomed to being on the receiving end of a no from anyone of the female persuasion obviously! It made her slightly glad she'd been able to spit out the rejection! So, she said it again, just to see his astonishment deepen.

"No," she said. "I can't. Santa does not date. Not until after Christmas."

Shoot. Was she leaving a door open?

His mouth twitched. "I'm not sure I would have called it a date," he said drily.

And her moment of pleasure at having surprised him disappeared. Of course he wouldn't call it a date! Anyone looking at him could tell he didn't need to go and buy fifty coats to get a date. Anyone looking at him could tell he didn't date girls like her.

He dated girls who had pierced belly buttons and tiny

diamond studs in their noses. He dated girls who were unself-conscious about rips in the derriere of their jeans. He dated girls who had gotten implants as their high school grad presents. He dated girls who were gorgeous, and self-assured, and who most definitely did not blush!

Even knowing she was the kind of girl he *never* dated, she felt the pull of the fantasy. What if she did say yes? What if over candlelight dinner she made him laugh and surprised him, and he found her so deep and rich in spirit that it made her totally irresistible despite the brown dress, worn sweater, lack of streaks?

What if he saw the princess under the Cinderella dressing? As if.

Insane thoughts, a flare-up of the child she had been at nineteen, before her nephew had been injured, the first broken link in a chain of events that led to the breakup of her sister's marriage. That breakup had left her stunned, confirming what her parents and James had already taught her, the lesson she had chosen to ignore. The very thing she had longed for most in the world—love—could turn back on you like a sharpened sword and pierce your heart.

Before that, despite evidence it was foolish, Kirsten had clung to the belief that she was a Cinderella of sorts, and that someday a prince would come who would see straight through the lack of breast implants and derriere-exposing jeans to who she really was.

"Well," she said brusquely, "Thanks. It was an amazing thing for you to do. I'm not sure why you did it, but I appreciate it. Now, I have a ton of work to do, so goodbye, Mr. Brewster."

He looked as if he hadn't even heard her. He moved by her and took one of the trike boxes down from the stack. He studied the drawing on the side of the box.

"You're telling me you know how to assemble this?" he asked.

She bristled! He was obviously used to a different kind of woman! One who worried about her fingernails and had never touched an Allen wrench or a crescent wrench in her life.

Of course, Kirsten had never actually assembled one of the trikes, though she had put together lots of other toys.

Still, honesty prevented her from claiming she knew how to assemble the trike.

"I can read directions," she said regally.

He yanked open the box, rifled through it, handed her the directions.

There were two pages of incomprehensible drawings, all clearly explained…in Japanese.

Her lips twitched, then she snorted, and then she laughed. She looked up to see the faintest smile toying at the edges of his lips, probably because of the snort!

"How about if we order a pizza?" he said, "and work together on the trikes?"

"Mr. Brewster—"

"Michael."

"I don't even know you."

He pondered that for a moment. "Are you scared of me?" Terrified!

"Do you want me to fill out an application? You can do a security check. I'll come back tomorrow."

It was the coming back part that terrified her.

"Don't be ridiculous," she said stiffly. She meant about him coming back tomorrow.

"It's not ridiculous. You should be checking out people who come to work here, even volunteers."

"I've been doing this for a long time without your help, thanks!"

"Hey, no need to get prickly! I was just trying to look out for you."

Which was her weakest point. She had grown up believing someday someone would look after her, forever, the way her father had looked after her mother. When her parents had divorced, she had been able to cling still to her dreams—though now they had been slightly tattered. Becky had found the most special man in the world, the baby had come and their love seemed to do nothing but become stronger and better.

And then it had all fallen apart. One second. A little boy in front of a car. A world shattered. A psychiatrist would have a field day with the fact Kirsten's interest in the fragile porcelain figurines had coincided with the breakup of something that had seemed stronger than steel.

"Hey," he said softly, "I'm offering to put together tricycles, not a peace agreement for the Middle East. Don't look so worried. You want a reference? You can phone my neighbor. That's who told me you might need help. Mr. Theodore."

"Mr. Theodore's your neighbor?" she said. "He sent you?"

"Suggested maybe I drop by. How do you know him?"

"We belong to the same book club."

"Book club. Whoo boy, I should have seen that one coming."

"Is there something wrong with girls who belong to book clubs?"

He actually grinned. "Yeah, they generally aren't dancing on the pool table at closing time with a rose between their teeth."

She should have been insulted, but it was a moment she had waited for without realizing she waited. That grin lit something in his eyes. For a moment she saw that there was fire trapped in all that ice. It glittered, wicked and warming.

She forgot to be insulted. His face, unhampered by grimness, was youthful and boyish and hinted at someone he had once been—full of mischief and laughter, easy-going charm.

"So, why exactly did Mr. Theodore send you looking for me?"

Something shuttered in his eyes, the moment was gone much too quickly. He shoved his hands in his pockets, shrugged. "I happen to have some time on my hands."

Yikes! How much time? And why would a healthy-looking young man have time on his hands to give to an organization like hers? Why wasn't he working? Involved with his own family at this busy time of year? But something told her, anxious as she was to find a flaw in him, not to ask. Not to press him. Not right now.

"Anchovies on the pizza okay with you?" She was aware it was a surrender of sorts. She wanted to get rid of him, really and truly. And yet his mystery pulled her, magnet to steel.

"Do the people in the book club even suspect that there is an anchovy girl in their midst?"

"Wild, isn't it?" she said drily. "Right up there with dancing on the table at closing time." And then, probably because it was getting late, and she was tired, and she'd employed her anti-blush technique so often she'd worn it out, she spoiled it by blushing at the very thought of dancing on any table, anytime.

And she knew it was the blush that made him laugh, and she wished Mr. Theodore had found somewhere else to send Michael Brewster at the very same time as being reluctantly aware that she was glad he had not.

That laugh gave her a glimpse, again, of what Michael had been once, and made her very aware he was not that now.

"Yeah, anchovies for me." He held her eyes for a moment, almost daring her to read the mysteries that were in his. And then he had the trike box dumped out on the ground and was contentedly pawing through about a million small pieces. She suspected even if the directions had been in English he would not have spared them more than the briefest of glances.

CHAPTER THREE

MICHAEL looked at the small purple tricycle with deep satisfaction. He attached the silver and white plastic tassels to each handlebar with a flourish—the final step in assembly—and took a step back.

"The tricycle king," he decided out loud. It was the second bike he'd put together. The first one had ended up with the handlebars on backward, but now he was pretty sure he had it down to a system. The rest of them were going to be a piece of—

"Pizza," Kirsten said, and came into the main room with a flat box, nicely grease-stained and wafting incredible aroma. "Sorry it took so long. The delivery guy said the roads are bad. Hey, that's cute."

He had the absurd masculine thought that maybe she was talking about his butt in blue jeans, but when he looked at her, she was regarding the trike with a look that made him feel big and confident and like he could assemble the Space Shuttle. For an understated kind of woman, he had the uneasy feeling she could make a man jump through hoops to make that admiring look appear on her face.

He decided hunger and the aroma coming off that pizza were two forces combining to make him a little bit more vulnerable than he wanted to be. Michael had managed to live in a world where he didn't need approval for quite some time, and he planned to keep it that way.

"It reminds me of something a chimp would ride at the circus," he said, and folded his arms over his chest. He wanted her to know the tough guy, not the trike king.

"Funny, isn't it, how we make associations? Trikes and chimpanzees. Cute."

That's not what he intended! Was she deliberately misunderstanding him? He slid her a look as she balanced the pizza on her hip, and used her free hand to shove the brand-new jackets down to one end of the table. She set the pizza down in the cleared spot. He frowned.

What was different? She wasn't quite as understated as before, that's what was different. She had lost the natty sweater somewhere, though he had not noticed it getting any warmer in this old drafty building. Not that he noticed things like that.

But his antennae were up, now. Without the bulk of the sweater, it was pretty hard not to notice her figure. For a delicately built woman, she had amazing curves in all the right places. Had she wanted him to notice?

Then he realized something else. She had put on lipstick. Not anything as bold as red—a kind of peach color, high gloss.

Speaking of associations, when a man looked at lips like that, he thought of one thing. And it wasn't eating pizza. His instincts had told him not to come back to this place, not to come back to her.

Of course, a police escort had a way of making a man ignore his instincts. But what on earth had made him ask her out for dinner? Had made him steamroll right over her refusal?

It was easy. Those tricycles had seemed like a better option than a night alone in front of his TV, and more loneliness than a man knew how to handle.

"Take a break," she said, and drew a pair of chairs up to the table.

He felt a certain reluctance to join her, probably because of the lipstick *and* the association and his acknowledgment of his own loneliness. Why had she put on lipstick?

For the same reason any woman put on lipstick, he deduced, and not happily. And it wasn't because it went well with anchovies, either.

No, it was to make a man notice her lips. And *associate*.

Which he did. For a book club kind of girl, her lips were at least as surprising as her figure—her lips were plump and sensuous, lips that looked as if a man did kiss them, she'd kiss back. She took an innocent bite of her pizza, as if she was totally unaware that she had succeeded in drawing his attention to her so completely. She closed her eyes with what seemed to him to be far more pleasure than a mere piece of pizza could deserve.

He took a gulp of his. Just as he thought, except for the anchovies, it tasted exactly like cardboard, a pizza completely unworthy of the happy little moaning sound she was making.

That sound had definite associations, too!

The name should have let him know he was in for a surprise or two. Not Molly or Sarah, nothing old-fashioned or sturdy about it at all. Kirsten. An uncommon name, that felt oddly familiar in his mind, as if he knew her well enough to know it suited her perfectly. He thought the name had a certain poetic quality to it, and he hated that he was even thinking about it at all. He had not spent one second contemplating Calypso's much more exotic moniker.

Perhaps it was just much safer to think about her name than

her lips, and the delicacy of the curves pressed into a white blouse. Which brought him back to her lips. She made a happy smacking noise.

"I think this is the best pizza in Treemont."

It was? He took another desperate bite of his pizza, hoping to fight off this strange weakness that was overtaking him. It was true. In a moment of clarity he realized the pizza was utterly delicious and that he could barely taste it. He looked longingly at the tricycles, glanced at her lips once more and with every ounce of strength left in him, he put the pizza down.

The woman's lips were an association that spelled one thing. Temptation. They made him feel hungry—and it was not a hunger a pizza could solve. They made him aware that he was lonely and empty, and they made him long to know if her taste, her touch, held salvation.

He wondered what those surprisingly luscious lips would taste like. Ripe peaches? Honey-kissed almonds? Maple syrup and smoke?

Anchovies, he chided himself. Still, he felt as if he touched them they would give him back something he had lost.

Insane to believe that!

If he kissed her on such a short acquaintance, she was the kind of girl who would probably hit him—which would be exactly what he deserved.

He realized he'd been playing the recluse for too long if a girl like this could be making him have thoughts like these ones. Maple syrup and smoke-flavored lips. The thoughts of a man becoming eccentric in his misery. As if his torture was not already complete, Michael remembered his earlier torment, the renegade thought of her fingernails on his back.

He looked at her hands. If he was not mistaken there was

a little clear gloss on the neatly manicured nails now, too. He was certain they had been unvarnished before.

A woman didn't take off her sweater, polish her nails and apply lipstick just to eat pizza! Even if a kiss was out of the question, she wanted him to notice her in *that* way.

"Well, I think I'll get back at it." He stood up, wiped his hands on his jeans, ignored her look of distress. "Trikes to build, forty days until Christmas." He had no idea how many days there were until Christmas.

"Thirty-nine," she corrected him automatically.

"Ah, even less time than I thought." He took a step away from her.

"Don't you like the pizza?" she asked, worried.

She'd admired his trike assembly, now she was *worried* that he wasn't getting enough to eat. Nobody had acted like that since his mom. Until this evening, he had been blissfully unaware that he missed being admired. He missed being worried about. He did not want to think of all the things a woman like her could make him so achingly aware he missed.

Despite the lipstick, that's the kind of girl she was: apple pie and ice cream, loved-little-kids-and-kittens, bring-her-home-to-meet-Mom. Except he no longer had a mom for her to meet. He felt that barbed sting: one of the ways he had disappointed his mother. He had never brought home a girl for her to meet. He felt a need, growing more desperate by the second, to disentangle himself from this situation that was causing these uncomfortable, wayward, painful thoughts. But it was going to be harder than he thought.

Kirsten's eyes were very wide on his face, and he had an ugly feeling she was also the kind of girl who would take it personally if he didn't like the pizza.

So he grabbed the whole piece and shoved it in his mouth, chomped, gulped, nearly choked and chomped some more.

She was looking slightly distressed over his barbarism, which he tried to convince himself was a good thing.

"I love the pizza," he managed to mumble, finally, when he'd managed to swallow it without strangling. But he knew a greater truth. He loved her lips. And she'd known he would! Lipstick. He was finishing the tricycles and then he wasn't coming back here, not for nothing.

With just the slightest effort, mousy Kirsten Morrison was making him weak. He needed so damn badly to be strong. How was he going to get through this season if he was not strong?

And wasn't strength to be untouchable? And didn't being untouchable mean to live in a haze where a man didn't notice lips? And worried looks? And cast-off sweaters?

"I'm not available," he said after he'd managed to swallow. "You should know that about me."

"Excuse me?" There was a slightly strangled note to her voice, too, but he soldiered on.

"I just thought you should know."

"Available for what?" she asked, a trifle shrilly.

"You know."

"No, I'm afraid I don't, Mr. Brewster. Maybe you could spell it out for me."

Mr. Brewster, that was good, a nice step backward from freshly applied lipstick. So, he continued to dig himself in.

"Well, earlier when I suggested dinner, you jumped to the date conclusion, and that's what I'm not available for." There! It didn't get any clearer than that.

"Maybe a man who is not available shouldn't be inviting

a woman out for dinner, not that I want to give the impression I care. You might remember I said no. Emphatically."

What was the point of pussyfooting around with a woman who tossed out a word like emphatically with such ease? This would be a lot easier if she never knew the power her lips held over him, if she just thought he was an arrogant ass, which of course he knew damn well he could be!

"Well, you did say no," he conceded uncomfortably, "but then you put on lipstick." He decided, given the fact the light in her eyes was becoming quite dangerous, it might be wiser to not mention he had noticed the disappearance of her sweater, or the nail polish.

"You thought I put on lipstick for *you?*" She got up so fast her chair fell over. Her hands balled and unballed. He could see the nail polish had looked clear but it really had a hint of pink in it. She had an unfortunate splash of tomato sauce on her blouse that he was pretty sure he was responsible for.

He realized she was surprising him again. He had thought she would blush and retreat when confronted about the lipstick. He had thought she would take his rejection like a little mouse, but he was looking at a tiger. A very angry tiger!

Unfortunately it just made him want to kiss her more than ever.

"Of all the gall," she spat out. "That is the most unbelievably arrogant thing I've ever heard!"

He thought maybe he was going to end up with a little tomato sauce on his shirt, too. Was she actually reaching for a slice of pizza? Did she think it would hurt if she threw it at him? No, she wouldn't be the kind of girl who was into hurting. Making a point would be more her style, though he doubted if she had ever made a point with pizza before. Now would be the wrong time to laugh. He knew that. This had all the makings of a crucial moment, one of those turning point places that had to be handled with care and sensitivity.

A caring and sensitive man, or even a man with more self-protective instincts would now apologize for his error—for the unbelievable ego it took to believe that makeup had been applied for his benefit—and back away from her.

But Michael had used up every ounce of his self-preservation months ago in the icy waters of the sea off the unforgiving coast of Alaska, and he never would have won points for sensitivity. He was aware he actually *wanted* to see just how surprising Kirsten could be, if she had what it took to throw the pizza at him.

"So, you put on lipstick to eat pizza?" he asked skeptically.

She went very still. He knew, instantly, he had not goaded her, as was his intention. He had hurt her. Kirsten did not pick up the pizza, and he knew darn well his callousness deserved the whole box dumped on his head. Instead, the anger drained from her face.

Her beguiling lip trembled, and she blinked hard.

He realized he didn't know what he was going to do if she started crying. He had wanted her to think he was an arrogant ass, not that *she* was defective. This was precisely why men like him did not end up with women like her. Kirsten was too sensitive. Giving in to the desire to taste her lips, ever, would be a disaster, tantamount to posting banns at the church.

"I didn't put it on for you," she said. "Ridiculous." Sniffle. "Anyone looking at me could tell a man like you would never think I was attractive no matter how much lipstick I slathered on."

This was going right off in the ditch. But if he told her, now, she was attractive it was going to sound insincere as if he was desperately backpedaling because of the tears. He chose a safer route. "Uh, it didn't exactly look like you *slathered* it on."

A tear squeezed out her eye and trickled sadly down her cheek. She scrubbed furiously at it.

He continued in a rush: "It didn't look slathered. Not at all." Tears stopped a man's brain dead, so he was pleased with the reassurance he came up with. "Dabbed!"

She did not appear reassured. "Your girlfriend probably models part-time for men's magazines, or at least for underwear ads," she said, and then made the whole miserable situation even worse by blushing and crying at the same time.

God, that girl had a blush that put Rudolph's nose to shame. Who blushed anymore?

"I don't have a girlfriend," he said, and then regretted it, for a little dishonesty would have been an easy out of this mess. A girlfriend. He could have gone back to building trikes—which he was finding surprisingly agreeable—without the complication of Kirsten painting her lips or moaning over her pizza.

"So," she said, backing away from him, her hand over her heart as if she had to protect it from him. "It really isn't about whether you're available or not. It's about whether or not you're available to a girl like me."

"No!"

"Pathetic book-clubber putting on her lipstick for the guy in the leather jacket and sports car with the green to-die-for eyes. The guy nice enough to buy fifty coats for needy children."

To-die-for eyes? His? She had to be kidding, though even he knew now wouldn't be the best time to press her on that.

"Kirsten," he said firmly, "You are not pathetic. Are you crazy?"

She nodded glumly. "Crazy and pathetic."

He said a swear word he was pretty sure they did not use at the Secret Santa Society or the book club. He took a step toward her, and she turned and bolted.

He reacted out of pure instinct. He went after her, took her shoulder, spun her around.

She looked like a kitten, hissing, getting ready to scratch. She jerked out from under his touch, but not before he had felt the suppleness of her skin, the richness of it, the softness of it.

He dropped his hand to his side and said evenly, straight from his heart, "Kirsten, it's got nothing to do with you. It's all about me."

"Why do I feel as if that's the story of your life," she said, and the haughtiness of her tone did not hide how much he had managed to hurt her. By noticing the damned lipstick, by being stupid enough to mention it.

See? He was out of practice at life, at social interactions. He had been breathing, surviving, nothing more. His pain was so great, it oozed out of him, and touched others, even when he didn't want it to.

But that did not give him the right to inflict pain, no matter how unintentionally, no matter how much they threatened the walls he had built around himself with their damned lipstick-painted lips!

Mr. Theodore was going to be so disappointed in him. He'd sent him here to help, and instead he was causing pain to someone who did not deserve it.

"Kirsten," he said, and something about the way he said her name stilled her, and him, too. His most hidden self was about to speak. He knew what was coming next, and he wished he could stop it, but he couldn't. From a long way away he heard his voice say, "I was in a terrible accident. That's why I'm not available."

"An accident?" she echoed.

Shut up, he ordered himself. He didn't tell anyone about that accident. Not anyone. He could not stand their pity, their platitudes. He could not stand it.

"I lost my whole world." *Shut up!* "My mother, my father, my brother. I have nothing to give anyone except pain, just like I gave you pain tonight."

Shut up. Please, please shut up. But his voice was going on and on, as if it had waited for this moment, like water waiting to burst out of a dam. "It's my first Christmas without my family. I don't know how I'll get through it."

His voice cracked, and was finally, blessedly silent.

She was silent for so long, and yet her silence was not uncomfortable. It was not her lips he was noticing now, it was her eyes. There was something in the dove-gray of those eyes that a man could hold on to, if he let himself.

Finally, when she spoke, she did not speak the words he dreaded. She did not say she was sorry, she did not ask what had happened.

She said, with unbelievable strength given her slight stature. "I know how you'll get through it."

Dumb to believe her. What did she know about his kind of grief? But somehow he did believe her, believed the quiet strength and calm in those eyes.

She wiped at her lips with her sleeve, as if she was trying to erase the fact she had ever wanted him to look at them. It was an admission.

The funny thing was it didn't change the pull of her.

Lipstick free, her lips were as compelling as they had been before. Maybe more so.

All he could see in her face was a lovely tenderness, compassion. He had hurt a woman who ran something called The Secret Santa Society. He was pretty sure he was going to hell for that.

And suddenly, he was aware he did have one small thing he could give her after all, that was not pure pain, one small thing to make amends for how he had just behaved toward her.

He could let her know she was a beautiful, attractive girl. That her lips had called him. Words would be useless, now. He had abused his right to use words to tell her anything that he expected to be believed.

He leaned toward her.

Predictably she took a step back. And then unpredictably, she took a step forward, reached up on her tiptoes and kissed him.

The kiss was a mere brush of his lips, butterfly wings against the petals of a flower. It was every bit as sweet as he had thought it would be.

And so much more that he was shocked. Her lips, smooth, silky, soft, had touched his for less than a full second, and yet he felt rocked, as if an earth tremor had moved through his world. He felt the walls he had built around himself so diligently, brick after careful brick, shift slightly, dangerously.

"Maybe," she said softly, her voice a balm and a caress, "you have more to give than you think. And that's how you'll get through it."

He wanted to insist he didn't, but something about that kiss had stolen his breath.

The purity of it, how it gave instead of took.

"What would you call those fifty coats if not giving?" she asked when he remained silent.

He shrugged it off, uncomfortable, took a step back from her, found his voice. "Oh. That. That kind of giving is easy."

"If it was that easy there would be no such thing as children who needed coats." She suddenly looked awkward. She looked at her watch. She blushed again, that incredible Rudolph's nose blush that could be a beacon on a cold, foggy night to a man who was lost.

To a man who had lost his soul at sea.

"I have to go now," she said abruptly, all business, afraid of this moment and the startling sense of intimacy they were sharing, just as he was. "I'm sorry. You'll have to leave, too. I don't have an extra key with me."

"I wouldn't let you walk out to your car alone, anyway."

She looked like she was going to protest, thought better of it. Oh, yeah, she was into letting him give now, even to her.

She turned back, scooped up the remaining pizza, packaged it neatly into a fridge that was tucked into a back corner.

A moment later, they opened the door, into the freezing night.

"Don't you have a warmer jacket?" she scolded.

Oh, sure now that he'd confided in her, she was going to treat him like an orphan. Worry about him. Be his mother, which was the last thing he wanted from her. He remembered she had worried about him before he'd confided in her.

"I don't get cold," he told her.

She shot him a puzzled look, but he was done with confessions for tonight. As she was locking the door, Michael noticed a large figure moving away from them down the street, shoulders hunched against a bitter wind.

"I think I saw that guy hanging out around your door before."

She turned. "Oh, him. He's always around. He's just a kid. I'm not sure who he is, but I think he thinks he protects me."

Michael looked at the young man moving away from them, and doubted the explanation for his presence was anything quite so altruistic, but it was a further insight into her that that was what she believed.

Innocent. She was innocent. Her lips had told him that, but even if they hadn't, her eyes had already said it.

But they had said something equally as dangerous: she was innocent. But that didn't mean she wanted to be.

They arrived at a car covered in snow. A small car, exactly what he would have expected her to drive. Practical, economical, nothing flashy.

Then again, who needed a flashy car when you had a secret weapon like her lips? She got in and started it, he wiped the snow off with his hands and the sleeve of his jacket, until she got back out and passed him a brush.

"Can I expect you back tomorrow to finish the trikes?"

He hesitated.

"It would be a big help."

But everything was so much more complicated now that he'd tasted her. He could just tell if he didn't come back she would make it about her instead of about him. That voice that kept talking, even when he told it to shut up, answered. "Yeah, sure, I'll be back tomorrow."

As Kirsten Morrison drove away, even though her car heater was not keeping up with the cold, she felt the distinct warmness of a woman who was playing with fire. Had she known exactly what she was playing with from the moment she had *dabbed* on that lipstick, removed the cardigan, applied the nail polish?

How humiliating to be seen through so quickly! A reminder of how dangerous his particular fire was—he understood women and how they thought, he had understood her motives even before she had completely sorted through them herself.

And to add a layer of complexity to everything, his terrible pain, his horrific loss. His whole family. Her heart felt as if it was breaking for him. Now, coupled with this unfathomable attraction, she felt a *duty* to help Michael Brewster make it through this Christmas season.

But how was she going to be in the same room with him now without thinking of that kiss? Without being swamped by fairy-tale dreams that went beyond kisses? That went to a future. A small house in a good neighborhood, nights of cuddling by the fire, babies...

"Stop it!"

That's what she got for kissing a stranger! Her motives had been stellar—to erase the sudden starkness that had appeared in his eyes. Or maybe they hadn't, because she had wanted to taste him, as if his lips would hold some truth she could cling to.

Her most treasured Little piece was *First Little Kiss*. It was the most valuable of her collection, because it was the oldest she owned, closest to the beginning of Lou's brilliant career. It showed Harriet and Smedley, leaning adorably close to each other, Harriet's lipstick marks on Smedley's cheek, eyes wide at what they had just done, tiny smiles of recognition on their faces, Smedley so obviously smitten, his eyes on Harriet's lips as if they were irresistible to him.

But kissing Michael had not been like that. The truth it had shown her was not about who Michael was, but about who she was, what secrets lurked in her. Something primal was in her, some longing and urgency that could totally capsize her controlled world.

Even more astounding, he had looked just as helpless, as if she wielded some power over him.

The *Little* piece somehow missed that. The *power*. The sizzle of playing with forces of nature that would not be controlled. *First Little Kiss* made it seem as if a little kiss was enough. It gave no indication that a kiss was a beginning, that it awoke deep longings, that it led somewhere else. She shivered just thinking about it.

Michael Brewster had warned her he was a man with nothing to give, and she knew when someone told you something like that it was a very wise thing to believe them.

But all her life she had been wise and practical—with the exception of the thousands of dollars she had spent on her *Little* collection—and suddenly she did not want to be wise and practical anymore. She wanted to be the kind of girl whose lips a man found irresistible.

More, she longed to be the one who healed what was broken in his soul.

She hit an icy spot on the road, and her car slid on the new snow, resisting her efforts to control it. She careened across the road, bumped up the curb and stopped only inches from a telephone pole. The items on her backseat fell on the floor. Thankfully, because of the lateness of the hour, there had been no oncoming traffic.

Her heart racing, she realized she had just been taught a lesson. She was on a slippery slope with Michael Brewster. She could lose control just that easily, and she could end up hurtling toward certain disaster with no ability to stop.

She shivered then scolded herself for being overly dramatic.

And for being way too afraid of getting hurt. It was unrealistic to expect to get through life with no bumps and bruises.

She thought of James, and the six weeks of heady wooing when she thought she had been in love. He'd known all the lines. *Slathered* her with affection and gifts and attention. And then, oh-so-casually, mentioned he was in danger of getting kicked off the football team without a better grade in math, and he'd figured out a way she could help him on the final. And it wasn't extra studying, either! She had cried herself to sleep for weeks. If a superficial, full-of-himself, manipulative guy like James could cause the kind of hurt he had caused her, what could Michael Brewster, a wounded grizzly bear, do?

"Put together a whole lot of tricycles," she told herself firmly. "Nothing more. He'll be bored inside of a week and he'll move on to the kind of things a man like that moves on to."

Underwear models came to mind. Safaris. Helicopters. High adventure of some sort. No, he was not the kind of guy whose interest would be held by tricycles for long, or by book-club kind of girls for that matter.

Meanwhile, her conscience would be clear. She would not wear lipstick. She would have done her part—everything in her power—to help him heal.

She snorted to herself. Had she really said to him, with such certainty, she *knew* how to get him through it? She had not even gotten through her own personal tragedies! How could she even think she knew anything about his?

No, in a week he'd be ready to go, and she'd be quite ready to say goodbye. A man like that would be just like too much egg nog—the first few sips were as heady as wine, and then it seemed too sweet, and then it was just sickening, and by the last few drops you wondered how come you ever thought you liked it in the first place.

She turned to make sure that her newly acquired catalog

had survived the slide off the backseat. But after shuffling through all the scattered papers, she realized she had forgotten it in her office. She frowned at that. Twenty-four hours ago she wouldn't have been parted from that brand-new catalog by a crowbar.

Had it been because he insisted on walking her to her car? Did she have an unconscious desire not to let Michael see her interest in the figurines? She hated that, that already she was trying to hide who she really was.

Or becoming something else, a little voice suggested.

He'd go. Of that she was certain. Michael would go and she would return to her fascination with the lovely, fantastic, *safe* world Lou Little had created.

But over the next few days, Michael did not get sick of putting together toys, nor was anybody treating him as if he was too much egg nog. No one even seemed curious about his availability, why a strong, healthy man had so much time to devote to them.

The volunteers just loved him unconditionally. Maybe they sensed the sadness in him, and knew to push him for details about himself would be to drive him away.

Kirsten was not even aware something had gotten stale at the Secret Santa Society until he came in like a breath of fresh air.

No wonder he knew what her lipstick had meant! Every woman who came through the doors, from age nineteen to ninety, flirted with him. Mrs. Henderson and Mrs. Jacobs were trying to outdo each other in the cookie department. Each day he was presented with shortbread cookies tenderly shaped into snowmen and Santas for him. Lulu Bishop, not to be left out of the action, had presented him with a Christmas cake so rum laden that Kirsten could smell it from her office. He'd been invited to all three houses for Christmas dinner.

Kirsten found it annoying. She was single. She was on her own. Not one offering of cookies or Christmas dinner for her. Of course, she had not confided in anyone that Becky and her nephew Grant, who had relocated to Arizona, had said they would not be able to afford the trip to Treemont this year.

And Kirsten had only been to see them once in Arizona, and had hated it there. She had thought she would find them unsettled and longing for home, instead she had to face how completely they seemed to be going on with their new lives, leaving all that was old behind them.

And Kirsten also found it annoying that she'd been so wrong about Michael Brewster. Even when he ran out of tricycles to assemble, he never seemed bored. He seemed content unpacking boxes, driving the cranky old truck to pick up donations, sorting through secondhand toys to see if they were salvageable, programming the odd computers that came in.

In a very short time, Kirsten didn't know how the Secret Santa Society had ever survived without him. How long it would be until she felt she could not survive without him, either?

CHAPTER FOUR

Thirty-three days until Christmas...

"MICHAEL, can you help with gift wrapping? I have to get some stuff into storage, we're running out of room in here."

He glanced up from assembling a wooden rocking horse. Kirsten had her long hair up in a clip, making a statement, just as she made one every day since he had started showing up here: girl *not* trying to attract a man.

Of course, the clumsy efforts she made were backfiring, the hair being up being a perfect example. Her bone structure was exquisite, delicate and feminine. Plus, there was nothing like a woman putting her hair up to make a man long to pull it down, to feel the silk of it run through his fingers. Okay, and maybe to wipe that look off her face, the one that said, *I did not kiss you. Or if I did kiss you it will be a cold day in July before it happens again.*

"Gift-wrapping?" He snorted. "That doesn't sound very masculine."

"Well, if your masculinity is so easily threatened, I'll ask someone more secure."

"Okay," he agreed, and smiled, challenging her to find someone else.

She glared at him. "You wouldn't believe the bottleneck that develops if we don't get toys wrapped and labeled. It is the job you don't want to leave until the ninth hour."

"I think that's eleventh hour." He had a gift for flustering her. He enjoyed it. She was just beginning to blush. With a small effort on his part, he bet he could get the full wattage.

"Look at these hands," he said to her. He moved closer to her and held them out for inspection. She looked, she blushed, her wonderful one-of-a-kind Rudolph blush that she seemed to save just for him.

Now, why did he have the feeling she wasn't imagining his hands gift wrapping? He pushed her a little. "I'm just not sure," he said smoothly, "that gift wrapping is the best use for these hands, Kirsten."

Her blush deepened, she sputtered, something about a fish!

"It's a rocking horse," he said, turning to see what part of the assembly he had screwed up enough for it to look like a fish. It looked like a horse to him. "And assembling rocking horses is," he injected his voice with as much innocence as he could muster, "the best use of these hands. My skills just wouldn't be fairly utilized in the gift wrapping department."

On the other hand, he had made a little deal with himself: he'd just take it one day at a time. After that first night of putting together tricycles, after kissing Kirsten, he'd gone home and thought *I can't go back there.* She was complicated...his feelings for her could become very complicated.

But here was the thing: he'd felt no desire to turn on his TV set, he'd felt no desire to have a beer. He was aware of feeling better—he couldn't say he felt good, but marginally better, as if he'd seen a promise of the sun through storm-blackened skies.

He'd asked for a life rope. He had asked in a moment of desperate honesty, *how will I survive?* He could not walk away from this *thing* that might be his answer.

He'd decided he would show up at the Secret Santa Society, even on those days when he didn't want to get out of bed, and do whatever was put in front of him. If it was gift wrapping, okay, he'd gift wrap.

The unforeseen bonus was giving Kirsten a hard time first.

So far, it was working out surprisingly well. He assembled toys, hefted the big stuff, drove the truck, hammered together extra shelving. He was *needed*, and he was busy, even busier than he had been at Mr. Theodore's, and it was a balm for his soul.

And he had the daily challenge of trying not to look at Kirsten's lips, and took some satisfaction from the fact she seemed to be trying just as hard not to look at his. It also gave him grave satisfaction that he could coax that blush out of her at least once a day and on good days, more.

She was not only not wearing lipstick in her campaign to erase that first night from his mind—or her own—she was wearing ugly sweat clothes, T-shirts from the thrift bin, too large jeans. The nail polish had disappeared from her fingernails, never to return.

The silent message, *I don't care what you think of me.*

She was a girl who couldn't lie, though. Her eyes said she cared, even though he'd warned her, fair and square, caring about him would be a risk.

Plus, her affinity for baggy wear had the unfortunate effect of making her look waiflike and adorable, extra small, the kind of woman an extra-large guy felt an instinctive, almost primal need to protect, to care for.

Today, she was wearing what he and his brother would have laughingly called mom-jeans and a bright red T-shirt that said in large letters stretched across her bosom, I Love Santa Claus. The outfit, on the ugly scale, rated a full ten.

Still, he was tempted to read the slogan very, very slowly, until she was nearly scarlet, and then lift his eyes to hers and say, "Do you want to come sit on my knee, little girl?" in his most wicked voice. He had to be careful, though. Kirsten had a way of surprising him, and she might do it, just as she had unexpectedly kissed him the other night.

And if he found the most adorable Kirsten Morrison on his lap, then what? He was pretty sure it wouldn't be, *Tell Santa what you want for Christmas*.

Even having thoughts like these—playful, teasing, slightly dangerous—was such a reprieve from the thoughts he had been thinking since a dark spring day all those months ago, that he felt grateful.

"Hey, what do you want for Christmas?" he said. That would be a nice, impersonal way to express gratitude for all the things he was getting here. Some clothes that fit her might make a good start. Was that impersonal enough?

"Getting all the packages wrapped by Christmas Eve delivery would be good enough for me."

A puppy, he thought. That would knock down her defenses. He'd love to see her melting and cooing over a little golden ball of fur. He bet she'd like a cocker spaniel. He reminded himself that he had helped her put her defenses up. Why would he want to knock them down? He was the one who had warned her he was not available.

Besides, a puppy was a wholesome kind of gift from a guy who thought wholesome kinds of thoughts. And Michael had been plotting for most of the morning how to catch a glimpse of a little something more than Kirsten wanted to show him. He thought there were probably nuns who showed more flesh than she did!

Of course, if he found a reason to make her have to reach the top shelf of the storage area—diabolical, he told himself. Unworthy of an emissary of Santa Claus.

"Mrs. Henderson said you can't have any of her special chocolate-dipped reindeer cookies unless you come wrap."

So, she wanted to play dirty?

"Okay, okay." He pretended to give in, knowing he could eat a whole lot of cookies before his wrapping skills were evaluated, deemed hopeless, and he was demoted back to wooden horse assembly.

"Uh, could you grab that game? Top shelf." He pretended to be engrossed with fastening the horse's surprisingly beady glass eye. "I think I saw a request for it on the board."

They posted requests as they came in on a board, tried to match them with incoming supplies. It was not the most efficient method, and if he was here long enough, he'd probably come up with something that actually worked.

How long did he plan to be here? His own answer surprised him. He had become a man who didn't make plans, who just got through each day as best he could. But somehow he knew he'd committed until Christmas. *Committed.*

He was distracted by the extreme discomfort of that thought when he noticed his ploy was working. Michael watched with evil delight as Kirsten spotted the game he claimed to want. Even when she pulled out the footstool, she had to stretch.

He was right. Bare skin. A taut tummy. A beautiful belly button. She could wear all the stupid clothes she wanted. He had an instinct for what was under there.

Diabolical, but you had to be careful working in a place like this not to be completely contaminated by the do-gooder stuff. A puppy, for God's sake! He was a man who bought women wine and sexy lingerie, gifts designed, really, with his own pleasure outmost in mind. He didn't want to become a saint, not that there was much chance of that.

She was still almost too short to get the game, she reached way up, stood on her tiptoes, managed to touch the game and lost her balance.

He was there in a flash, put his hands around her waist, swung her down onto the floor. He didn't let go right away, and for a moment she didn't move.

Here was the problem: he thought he was playing with her, but he had awakened that hunger within himself—to touch, to feel softness, to connect. His hands nearly spanned her waist. She smelled, ever so subtly, of gardenias.

"All hands to gift wrap!" The public address system was old, and sound crackled, burped and exploded out of it. He and Kirsten snapped apart as though they were teenagers caught in a cop's spotlight in the back of a car.

Not that she had probably ever been in the backseat of a car, something he needed to remember when he was aching to touch her skin again!

He followed her to gift wrap, two long tables set up with bows and tape and tags and wrapping paper. The regulars were all there, his wonderful substitute moms. He glanced at the platter of cookies. It would take him about fifteen minutes to polish those off and then—

The music started. "No!" he protested. "I can't handle it. I'm begging. Really."

So, he wasn't the only one who enjoyed the odd evil moment. The old gals were all snickering happily at his complaining.

They liked the traditional Christmas tunes, whereas he preferred something a little more modern.

"What do you want to listen to?" Kirsten asked. Sheesh. She was still blushing!

"Something contemporary. Some rock music perhaps."

She actually produced a tape. All the women were smiling benevolently at his expression. His requests for rock and roll had been falling on seemingly deaf ears since he'd arrived.

Since he'd arrived. Almost a week had gone by already. It was the first time since the accident that time seemed to be moving with any speed at all.

All these women mothering the hell out of him. It was as if he had arrived at an oasis after traveling across the burning sand. They were water to his thirst.

Michael Brewster wasn't a man given to any kind of fancy. He did not believe in anything flaky. Reality was what you could touch and taste, smell and feel. When people tried to comfort him with platitudes about angels watching over him, he felt angry rather than comforted.

And yet there was something here he could not explain, a *feeling* of his mother's presence. Probably only because these women were so much like her: they frowned when he swore, and forgave instantly when he muttered his apologies. They baked him cookies and casseroles, he'd had offers to mend his jeans, and he didn't know how he was going refuse all those Christmas dinner invitations without hurting someone's feelings. Mrs. Jacobs had offered to come to clean his house!

"How do you know my house needs to be cleaned?" he'd asked her.

"Oh, I just know," she'd said, with a smile so like his mother's had been when she'd seen his first very messy apartment.

So even though he was pragmatic to a fault, Michael sometimes wondered if his mother someway, somehow, using angel tricks, had led him to this place where so many women were so eager to mother him.

Now this.

A classic song by one of his favorite artists filled the room, making Michael aware he had been holding his breath and crossing his fingers that what they had chosen wouldn't be something awful. He let it out in relief, and felt suddenly warm.

Really warm.

Was he flushing?

Good God, a week ago he could count on himself not to feel cold—or warm. And not to blush, either. He should just turn and walk out of here. No, run. Run from what was happening to him, the slow, aching return of feeling, of a desire to hope and believe that life might be good again.

But if he ran they would be so dismayed—so worried about what they had done wrong—and they all looked so pleased with their little conspiracy to surprise him with his favorite music.

"Now that's music I can gift wrap to," he said, not letting on that ice inside him was melting faster than ice cream under a hair dryer. He put his hands over his head and did a little thing with his hips that usually could get him a girl at closing time.

Mrs. Henderson gasped then threw her adhesive tape at him. Mrs. Jacobs chortled. All three hundred pounds of Lulu quivered. And Kirsten was looking down at the package in front of her, gift wrapping with manic fervor.

"Want to dance, Kirsten?" He was teasing her, and he wasn't. He wanted to touch her again.

"No!" She did not look up.

"I will!" Lulu said. And so he danced with Lulu and then Mrs. Henderson and then Mrs. Jacobs, to the nice mix of not-Christmas music they had put together for him.

No, not they. Not one of these women would have chosen anything more recent than Frank Sinatra. So, this was a gift from Kirsten, who was sternly ignoring him, and muttering about the urgency of the gift wrapping task at hand.

"Kirstie," he said, using, for the first time, the shortened form of her name others used all the time, "Come on."

"No."

But the grannies were having none of it, and Lulu used her considerable bulk to coerce Kirsten away from the table.

"You dance with him!" she ordered.

Kirsten stood in front of him, defiant. She folded her arms over her Santa T-shirt and tapped her foot. "If we could just get on with the gift wrapping—"

She was soundly booed by her volunteers. The music changed. A broken, mournful voice filled the room, crackled over the terrible speaker system, singing about a beautiful woman.

"May I have this dance?" he asked, his voice low, suddenly aware how much he wanted her to say yes, how he wanted to feel her skin beneath his hands again.

"No."

More boos.

"Come on, Kirsten," he teased her, "loosen up."

"I don't want to loosen up," she hissed, for his ears only. "I can just imagine what happens to women who loosen up around you."

"Can you?" he said. "Dirty mind."

"Oh!"

"All the other girls danced with me," he pointed out to her.

"That's the whole problem. For a guy who is unavailable, you're a little too sure of your attractions. Why, there's a name for guys like you!"

"And what is it?"

"You know darn well what it is."

"I don't," he said stubbornly.

"You're a…a tease." She was keeping her voice down—way down—but if any of those gals caught a glimpse of her face they would assume she was saying much naughtier things than she was.

Though for a girl like her to call a guy a tease was probably plenty naughty.

"They have a name for girls like you, too."

She glared at him.

"Pure as the driven snow," he said, but it didn't come off his lips sounding anything like an insult.

"By your standard!"

It had been so long since he had felt like this: light, energized. Dare he say happy?

"Hey, I'm just a brokenhearted guy, looking for a moment's haven," he said. He had meant it to come out sounding the way he thought he felt: happy. But it didn't. Not at all. It sounded like it came from a place within him that had not seen light for a long, long time.

She faltered. He had just played the broken heart card to

manipulate her to dance with him. It seemed a shabby thing to do, until the moment his hand touched hers.

Something that was ravaged within him stilled. A place of darkness was pierced by a shaft of light. He had known it would feel like this from the moment he had lifted her down from that stepstool, he had known even then, he had to feel this way again.

That was the possible problem with working for the Secret Santa Society. Miracles happened here. A man's shabbiest moments could bring unexpected gifts.

Somewhere, from a long time ago, dance class in PE, he remembered how it was supposed to be done. As much as he wanted to pull her in tight to him, and hang on to the way she was making him feel as if he would never let go, he couldn't. You couldn't just slam a girl like Kirsten up against your chest and hold her so close that there was nothing between you, not even air.

No, he took one of her hands, put his other hand lightly on her waist, missing the sensation of her bare skin under his hand, but trying to be satisfied. He kept enough distance between them for Lulu to slide into if she wanted to.

To his amazement rather than appreciating his effort at chivalry, Kirsten looked annoyed. "This is how you would dance with your grandmother."

If Michael had hoped dancing with someone as pure as the driven snow would be like dancing with his grandmother, formal and stiff, a duty, a moment that could erase the hunger from him, he'd been mistaken.

Kirsten could be counted on to surprise. He had expected she would be stiff as a board to dance with, uptight. Only she wasn't. She moved with ease, an unexpected sensuality that was easing the hunger in him at the same time it was making it worse.

"You don't know how to dance!" she accused after a few steps.

"I'm trying to remember. Grade eight dance class."

"You're telling me you haven't danced since the eighth grade?"

"Not like this."

"How do you usually dance?"

He thought that might be an invitation. He thought of her arms draped around his neck and her lithe body pressed into his every place two bodies could touch. He thought of his lips on her ears and her throat. Desperately he tried to ignore his own thoughts, and her invitation, and recount his eighth grade dance adventures instead.

"I had to dance with Millie Milesworth. She was smarter than me, and held me in complete contempt."

"Would that be because you tormented her?"

"Why are you taking her side? You don't even know her."

"I'm not taking her side. I just know she was only pretending not to like you so you wouldn't hurt her too badly."

Ah. Would that be the same as wearing baggy clothes so that a man would think you didn't care what he thought? Women were so damnably complicated.

"How would you know something like that about someone you'd never met?" he asked.

"Hmph. I was probably her. And you were probably James Moriarty."

"Why do I have the sinking feeling he was a jerk?"

"Ouch."

Her foot felt small and fragile underneath his. "Sorry. Was he a jerk?"

"Yes, he was."

"Was he mean to you?"

"Yes."

"I'll track him down and look after him for you." He was surprised at how much the thought pleased him.

"Thanks, but I'm mature enough not to let college slights still bother me."

The change in her body language as soon as she had mentioned James Whoever told him that was a complete lie, though he refrained from calling her on it.

"Plus, that's not exactly in keeping with the spirit of the season."

The standard line around here: it addressed wayward swear words, yelling at the truck driver who was late and other forms of manly behavior. Sometimes he longed for a good barroom brawl.

"Why? What do you think I'd do if I met old James in a dark alley?"

"Oh, something male and brutish."

"In defense of your honor! You should be pleased." He was getting the hang of this dancing thing. Relaxing. He liked the way her hand felt in his hand, how the other one rested on his shoulder. He remembered how his mother and father used to look dancing, as if they heard the very same music at the very same time, felt the very same things.

He got carried away, attempted a dip in their limited space, knocked over a pile of teddy bears, nearly dropped her on the floor and had to let her go.

She looked like she'd escaped the mouth of death. He knew that the dance was over. Just like Millie, he could see it in her face. She was scared he would hurt her too much.

And he probably would. Too many empty places inside

him that nothing could fill. Not even the sweet, sweet love of a girl like her.

"You know what would please me?" she said. Her voice was shaking slightly. "Getting the wrapping done."

He bowed. "Yes, ma'am," he said, knowing better than to put up a fight, feeling an unwanted tug of regret. What if he had met her before it happened? Before he had been separated from all that mattered to him by forty-foot seas?

Probably he would have overlooked her for the flashier model. This ability to see qualities in a woman beyond a D-cup seemed to have been born as a direct result of his own suffering. He'd never been anything before but the most superficial of guys, looking for a good time, no strings attached.

He was very much aware Kirsten had turned the tables on him again. Dancing with her was not what he'd expected. She had fit with him. She had not seemed too small, and he too large. She had seemed feminine and supple and graceful. And totally alluring.

"What do you want for Christmas?" he asked again, before she made good her escape, seeing something vulnerable in her eyes.

He could get her a nice gift since his heart was all used up and he couldn't give her damaged goods.

"An elf," she said, quickly, "You promised me an elf. If you can find me an elf, I'll be happy forever."

And it wasn't until she said those words that he realized a startling truth.

Even though she was at the center of this incredible hub of activity, even though she appeared busy and full of purpose, even though she was needed and admired and loved by all these volunteers, even though she was surrounded by magical toys and making wishes come true, the most noble of causes, Kirsten Morrison was unhappy.

Looking into her eyes at that moment, he knew her deepest secret: she dreaded Christmas. More than he did.

The thing Kirsten hated most about Michael Brewster was how he was looking at her now, as if he could read the secrets in her soul.

No, that wasn't quite it. The thing she hated most about him was how, even though he was a man in pain, he could make Mrs. Jacobs laugh out loud, and Lulu Bishop wiggle, and Mrs. Henderson talk about the husband who had died last year.

The thing she hated most about him was how he could get a donation that she had tried to get for months, simply by turning up the wattage on that slow, sexy smile of his.

The thing she hated most about him was how he could make her blush by simply looking at her for too long. The thing she hated most about him was how, before his arrival, each day had always unfolded very much like the last one, and suddenly she was dancing down the teddy bear aisle, feeling oddly, woefully, as if her life had just begun, as if she'd been born to dance with this man.

The thing she hated most about him was, just when she thought he was the most annoyingly confident tease in the universe, she would see that faraway look in his eyes, see how the ice was still there, and sorrow. She would see just how hard he would be to love. And how easy.

He really wasn't available. And what she hated about him was that when they danced, when he teased her, when he looked at her, when he touched her with those hard, work-worn hands, it seemed as if he was. Or should be. Or could be.

He better not really be getting her a gift! It would be a pity present, because when he looked at her she felt as if her every secret yearning was being broadcast out loud.

He looked like the kind of guy who might buy his women lingerie and decadent chocolates and effervescent wines. Not that he'd buy her that. No, she probably fell into the Millie Milesworth category: something impersonal, like those boxed mitten and hat sets that came out at this time of year.

She would never, ever tell him the truth, that what she truly wanted, if she could have anything in the world, was a limited edition figurine called *Knight in Shining Armor*. She was sure he would find her *Little* collection pathetic. Laughable.

"She wants *A Little Puppy Love*," Lulu said at the exact moment Kirsten had decided her love of everything *Little* was something she was keeping to herself.

Kirsten glared at her. The volunteers always chipped in together and got her one of her cherished figurines. Lulu missed the glare because she was, tongue out, trying to get a delicate ribbon to cooperate with her beefy hands.

"What?" Michael said, and laughed. He had no idea what *A Little Puppy Love* was, so how could his laugh hold derision?

"Ahem." Lulu looked up, Kirsten swiftly drew a finger across her own throat.

"Nuthin'," Lulu said sulkily. "I didn't say nuthin'."

"Come on, Lulu," he said, all charm and persuasion. "Tell me what she wants."

"Well, I thought I knew but I guess I was mistaken," Lulu said huffily. "I'll return the volunteers' donations to them."

Kirsten was going to lose an opportunity to add *A Little Puppy Love* to her collection? Because of him? It was worth it. She did not want him to know about her fascination with all things *Little in Love*.

"I knew you'd like a puppy," he said with satisfaction.

"I'm allergic to dogs," she shot back with equal satisfaction.

Now that he'd brought up the whole gift thing, Kirsten was wondering if she was obligated to give him a gift. She certainly didn't want to. Shopping for him would be a nightmare of trying to appear thoughtful but not smitten.

She always got all the volunteers a small gift, a token of her appreciation. She wished she'd been generic in past years: good quality chocolates, nice bath oil. Oh, no, she'd had to prove how much everyone meant to her by matching the perfect gift to them. So Lulu got the imported silk scarf, and Mrs. Henderson got the cranberry glass to add to her collection, Mrs. Jacobs got a gift certificate for a turkey to help her with the monstrous number of people she fed every year, Mr. Temple got socks with little heaters in them.

So, what did you get a man like Michael Brewster?

A new leather jacket? Too expensive. Some good old rock and roll CDs? He probably had a substantial collection. Maybe, on a lighthearted note, a certificate for some dance lessons.

Maybe you'd get *him* a puppy to try to fill the hole in his heart—a little ball of fur that would grow enormous, a St. Bernard or a Great Pyrenees.

If he was her man, she'd fill his sock with little treasures, with an MP3 player loaded with love songs that would embarrass him, homemade fudge, funny underwear.

He wasn't her man, she reminded herself. He had warned her about him. Even if he hadn't, *she* didn't want a man, she didn't want love.

It was too easy to forget that it started like this: yearning for his smile, his eyes to linger on her. And then those yearnings grew: now they included this desire to know if they danced together often enough what it would become. It started with puppies and love songs and kisses, loving gestures and kind thoughts.

And one second could change everything. That's how fragile it was. Except in the Little Love world where love stood still, and was always fresh and delightful and full of exquisitely tender moments, captured, never to change.

Michael had moved back to the gift wrapping table. He had managed to make a perfectly square box that contained a jigsaw puzzle look like a wrinkled elephant constructed out of wrapping paper.

Love would make that seem so cute. If Lou Little could see it, he'd probably make a figurine out of it. *Love's Little Gifts.*

That's what she hated about Michael Brewster.

"Where are the tricycles?" he asked. "I want to wrap the tricycles."

He said it as if he was pleased with the mess he'd made of the puzzle, and now he was confident about tackling bigger things. That was the ego of the man, never mind love's little gifts!

"We don't wrap the tricycles," she told him. "They're too hard. They take too much paper. We just put a bow on them."

"But you deliver them Christmas Eve?"

"Yes."

"But then some poor little kid knows what he's getting. I mean, Christmas for little kids is about lying awake, anticipating what's inside that big lumpy parcel. And think about nothing to unwrap the next morning. Unwrapping! It's the spirit of Christmas. Tearing paper! Making a mess. Dying to see what's inside that package."

See? That's what Kirsten hated about him. Even though he had survived his own personal hell, even though he wanted to have a hard heart, he could still *feel* what every child wanted on Christmas morning.

"Michael," Lulu said appreciatively, "you could talk a virgin into skinny dipping."

Mrs. Henderson clucked disapprovingly.

"I certainly hope so," Michael said.

Kirsten was wrapping as if her life depended on this board game being covered. *He better not be looking at me,* she thought. *Kirsten don't you dare give him the satisfaction of looking at him to see if he's looking at you.*

She peeked. He wagged his eyebrows at her. He was the man least likely to ever inspire a figurine. Imagine. *Love's Little Skinny Dipping.* Unfortunately she could imagine it, and all too clearly, but it wasn't Harriet and Smedley she was imagining it with. She closed her eyes, conjured a picture of raw squid, felt the heat recede.

But when she opened her eyes, he was looking at her with *knowing* eyes. She could see he was making assumptions about her! And very personal ones, too. No matter that it happened to be true. In fact, that just made it all worse.

There it came. She could feel it. *Squid, squid, squid.* Too late. The heat moving up her face would not be stopped. He delighted in tormenting her, in making her blush. And he was good at it, too.

That's what she hated most about him.

"Oh, give me a damned tricycle," she said.

"That's the Christmas spirit," Michael said approvingly.

CHAPTER FIVE

Twenty-five days until Christmas...

MICHAEL BREWSTER could never have seen this one coming. Christmas wrapping had become the bane of his existence.

Ever since he'd insisted on wrapping the tricycles, every odd shaped and overly sized gift in the place was presented to him. Three-foot teddy bears, snowboards, horses-on-springs, they were all his department now.

Currently, he was scratching his head over a pink child's two-wheeler bicycle with training wheels.

A group of people so different had probably rarely been assembled at the same table, he thought as he settled into the task. Black, white, old, young, thin, fat, male, female.

And then there was Kirsten. Her commitment to looking as unappealing as was possible seemed to be relaxing over the last few days. Today she had on a cute pair of hip-hugging jeans, and a zip-up hooded top over a T-shirt that looked like it fit. If he was not mistaken, her lips had the tiniest bit of shine to them.

He didn't even want to contemplate what that meant, but it did seem strange to him, the more he got to know her, that she was not taken. She could be intensely funny, she was cute, she was intelligent, and as a complete bonus, she had a fine figure.

Of course, she had a tendency to be a bit too serious and she did have the weird interest in those awful figurines. After Lulu had let it slip that day, he had looked up *A Little Puppy Love* on the Internet. After spending a hopeless evening sorting through Donny Osmond songs, and dog kennels, he'd taken Lulu aside and gotten the true scoop—plus parted with twenty bucks toward Kirsten's gift from the volunteers.

Then it had been back to the Internet, because even though Lulu had assured him that the volunteers had *A Little Puppy Love* covered, he'd been intrigued about why Kirsten didn't want him to know what she really wanted for Christmas.

In no time flat, Michael had been introduced to the whole horrible world of *Little in Love*. Smedley, with that smarmy expression on his face, and that toothpick slenderness was cartoonish and insipid, and Harriet had had the same vapid, unchanging expression on her face since 1957.

He hoped Kirsten's interest really was about the puppy in that particular figurine, since she couldn't have a real one, poor girl, but his antenna were up. The next day he couldn't help but notice she had a *Love's Little* collectible in her office called *Love in a Little Canoe*. Worse, she appeared to have a catalog, that she quickly snapped shut anytime he was around.

But despite that enormous fault, the fact she liked those idealistic and unreal 3-D portraits of what love should look like he truly couldn't figure it out. Why would a girl like her be alone?

Alone.

He glanced around the table one more time and realized that was the common denominator among all the volunteers.

Lulu was separated, Mrs. Henderson recently widowed,

Mrs. Jacobs had lost her husband long ago, Mr. Temple had never been married. He knew they all had plans for the big day—families or friends they would be with on Christmas—but that, just like him, they were looking for a way to get through it. Each person in this room had looked beyond themselves to find someone who *needed*. Who was in more pain than they were.

Here behind the doors of the Secret Santa Society, a family had been born.

And he had been accepted into that family with open arms.

He had a sense of epiphany, of having a mission here that was larger than providing his brawn, larger than being placed in charge of wrapping the bulkier packages, larger than the impossible task of trying to unearth a Christmas Eve elf. It was larger than his own healing.

It was larger, even, than looking at Kirsten's lips, and larger than thinking of new and innovative ways to make her show him her tummy or blush.

Though since he was thinking of that blush, he decided to stare at her newly glossed lips until she noticed he was staring.

She did. "Chapped," she told him, not a blush in sight.

She was getting just a little too good at turning the tables on him!

"If you could have anything you wanted for Christmas," he asked, trying to let her know how absolutely serious he was by scowling at her playful expression, "what would it be?"

"Every kid in this neighborhood to get a gift delivered *and* an elf," Kirsten said. Trust her to ignore his scowl, and to move it away from the personal.

"I wasn't asking philosophically. I meant materially."

"That figures," she said, but she softened it by grinning at him, showing him that flash of her that was full of mischief and spunk. It wasn't really lipstick, but he didn't think it was lip balm, either. Gloss.

"Mrs. Hennie-Pennie," he said, ignoring Kirsten since she had decided her latest dance step would be the sidestep, "What about you?"

Mrs. Henderson was pensive. Finally, she said, "You know what I'd like for Christmas? German chocolates. My Addie sent me home some when he was stationed over there. Before we even got married. Then every year, I don't know how, he got me some. They come in a thin box, called Merci—" she pronounced it *murky* "—a French name for German chocolates. I swear I wake up with a longing for that taste in my mouth, sometimes. Thinking of him. Missing him."

They were all very quiet, and then Lulu broke the silence.

"Me, I want one of them home spa things you put your feet in, and warm water massages your tired tootsies. Don't that sound like heaven? And not nearly as much trouble as a man." She laughed robustly, and Kirsten joined in with more enthusiasm than he thought the comment warranted.

As their laughter faded, his mission clarified suddenly, he could see it as if a light shone on it, brilliant as that star the Wise Men had followed.

He was here to be the secret Santa for the Secret Santa Society. He could get each of these goodhearted volunteers, who did so much and expected so little, the Christmas gifts of their dreams.

Mrs. Henderson could have a crate of murky chocolates, and he could get Lulu a weekend at the best spa in Michigan. No, maybe he'd send her to that luxury one in Arizona. His mother had kept a brochure and he'd found it, unexpectedly, in with the pizza menus. He liked the thought of that—Lulu going to a place his mother had quietly dreamed of, and never once mentioned.

Mrs. Jacobs wished her son who was overseas could come home with the grandchild she had yet to see. Michael took mental notes as each woman spoke, he could feel the warmth growing in him as if somebody kept cranking the thermostat in this place.

Just a few short weeks ago, he had been a man who could not feel temperature. Now it felt as if he was going to have to rip his shirt off any minute, he was so warm, so on fire.

He could just imagine Kirsten's eyes going all round—and hopefully awed—if he did that.

"What about you?" he asked her, finally, when each of those women had explored her Christmas fantasies thoroughly. "Kirsten?"

"I told you," she said uncomfortably. "An elf."

"No, I'm serious."

"Okay," she said sharply. "Serious. A dancing hippo with a pink tutu."

Everyone laughed, except him. He realized she had deflected his question. She didn't want anyone to know what she wanted for Christmas.

"I know you like those figurines," he said. *"Little in Love."* It actually hurt to say it, it sounded so stupid.

"How do you know that?" she snapped.

"Well, Lulu mentioned it the other night, before you shut her up by threatening to cut her throat. How's that for Christmas spirit?"

She was glaring at him, but silent.

"You have one of those things in your office. And a catalog."

So, if she said which one she wanted, instead of sitting

there with a mulish look on her face, Michael figured he'd suck it up and get it for her, even though it went seriously against his grain.

This was part of his epiphany: Christmas wasn't about doing what made *you* happy, though he remembered fondly the time he and Brian had pooled their money to buy their mother a silver-plated .22 rifle. Never once had she acted as though she was anything but delighted, and she had generously lent it to them whenever they asked for squirrel and gopher hunting.

Kirsten, however, seemed bent on making his mission difficult.

"I don't want anything from you," she said a little stiffly.

He might have been insulted, only when he looked at her, he wondered if she wanted anything at all. Maybe—hopefully—*Little in Love* was just a smoke screen, something to ask for because she couldn't think of anything else. It struck him as a strange and sad irony that this young woman, so determined to give Christmas to everyone else, somehow did not truly believe in the season. She could give but not receive.

Except Michael Brewster made it his mission, right then and there, to find out Kirsten Morrison's heart's desire and to make sure she got it—whatever it was—for Christmas.

So, he pretended he hadn't heard her say she didn't want anything from him. "Come on," he chided her. "Spill it. You must want more than *Love's Little Doggy Breath, Love's Sloppy Kiss* or *Love's Little Honeymoon from Hell.*"

He was cracking up at his own cleverness when he noticed she wasn't laughing, and realized she really did like those truly ridiculous figurines, and he'd only set his own quest to find out what she wanted back by mocking her. Should he just get her a couple of those blasted things and be done with it?

The thought made him shudder.

But over the next few days, it seemed the more he pursued it, even with all the *sensitivity* he could muster, the more determined she became not to tell him anything about herself.

"So, Kirsten, have you thought about what you want?"

"I was up all night thinking of nothing else."

He glared at her, knowing he was about to get a taste of his own mockery thrown back at him. "And?"

"World peace," she said, that hint of mischief again.

"Are you running for the Miss America pageant? The stock answer."

She laughed. "Yeah, girl most unlikely to be Miss America."

"More the shame, that," he muttered.

"Right."

"No, really," he said stubbornly, and meant both that it was a shame a girl like her would never be Miss America, and that he really wanted to know what she wanted for Christmas.

He tried a different tack. "So, what are your hobbies, when you aren't here?"

Not subtle enough. She smiled at him, and he braced himself. More payback mockery coming. "I read books. B-o-o-k-s."

"Hey, just because I'm a dumb carpenter, doesn't mean I'm dumb."

She was so green to the whole teasing thing that she spoiled it all by looking sincerely abashed. "I'm sorry. I didn't mean to imply that."

Good. A weak moment. "I'll forgive you if you'll tell me."

For a moment, he thought he'd made headway.

"You tell me first," she countered. "What do you want for Christmas?"

The question took him by surprise. What did he want for

Christmas? He realized the answer was nothing. He was wealthy. Anything he wanted he could buy.

And yet there was nothing he could buy that he wanted.

What his heart ached for was his family. Unbidden his mind crowded with memories. The ridiculously large tree his mother insisted on every year, so big they could barely get it in the front door. The gag gift he always got from his brother. His father's excitement about how he planned to surprise his mother.

The highlight of Christmas morning, though Michael had not recognized it at the time, was not his own pile of gifts, but the last gift of the morning. His father waited until every other parcel was opened, and then with great ceremony, he would hand his gift to his wife.

Open it, Eileen, open it, his voice betraying his anxiety and his excitement that he had gotten it just right. Of course, Michael realized only now, she was a woman who could seem to love a rifle. Those big emerald earrings she'd gotten one year could not have possibly been to her taste. Another year, when they had had a particularly good take on the crab boat, there had been a diamond necklace.

Always, even when the year had been lean, that final gift was something foolishly extravagant. Michael remembered his mother's mouth forming that "O" of surprise, her eyes filling with tears, her looking at his father with such tenderness, such tenderness…

"Michael, what is it?" He came back to the here and now, to find himself being regarded with gentle concern. Kirsten's hand was on his wrist, reminding him how much he liked her touch, reminding him he wanted to dance with her again…

"Nothing," he said, and then had to get away from that look in her eyes, any way he could. "What was the question?"

He was fighting for time to regain his composure.

"What do you want for Christmas?" She was watching him way too carefully, her hand was still on his wrist. How could so much strength come from such a tiny hand? How could such a light touch fire such yearning in him?

"A beautiful woman," he said, wanting to annoy her, and hopefully make her blush.

Only she didn't. She regarded him steadily. "Santa will have trouble getting that in your sock," she said.

She did remove her hand, though.

"He can leave her on the doorstep. Your turn."

"If the moon's made out of blue cheese, I want a piece of it."

"Look, for such a simple question, you are really having trouble with the answer."

"You, too!"

"One. Simple. Answer."

"I'm complicated," she said sweetly.

"No kidding."

Well, playing Santa for her might mean playing a little dirty then. The next time she left to run an errand, he slipped into her office.

Just as he suspected, it was a *Little in Love* catalog that was quickly stuffed into her top drawer every time he came anywhere near her office. It was worse than he thought. *A Special Collectors' Catalog*. One page was pathetically well-worn. *Knight in Shining Armor*. Michael thought it was possibly the worst of the *Little in Love* collection to date.

The page informed him that piece was a limited edition. Only two thousand of them would be cast and Special Collectors, whatever the heck that was, would have first dibs on every single one of them. He had the sinking feeling it was not simply a sales pitch that *Knight in Shining Armor* was expected to sell out within days of being offered. He flipped to the front of the catalog, checked the date. Which meant it was probably already sold out.

It made his head hurt that two thousand of these were going to be released on the world. It made his head hurt that everything she wanted was always difficult. The elf was proving impossible and now this.

Wasn't this something that someone much older than her should collect anyway? He pictured an old crone of about ninety, with cats crawling all over her lap.

Michael was willing to bet not a single collector of *Little in Love* was a man. Because men simply did not think like this.

"*Knight in Shining Armor*," he scoffed. Real men were more for nights of sweating amour. No wonder she didn't want to tell him what she wanted for Christmas. It was an embarrassment to her, as well it should be. Still, his Christmas list was now complete. He knew what she wanted, and nothing was impossible. He felt optimistic, happy even.

But the thing about happiness was that you couldn't trust it. And he was about to close her desk drawer when his gaze fell on something else. Slowly he picked up a file marked Impossible Dreams. Kirsten's impossible dreams?

Reluctantly he flipped open the file, and found out some things were impossible after all.

"What on earth are you doing?" Kirsten asked, incensed. She was not even sure why she asked. It was quite evident that Michael was quite at home in her seat, in her office, reading her papers.

He looked up at her, as if he had no idea he shouldn't have made himself at home at her desk.

It was just wrong that he could make her feel uptight when he was the one in the wrong!

"Kirstie," he said, "is your heart broken?"

Her breath stopped. What had he found in her desk that had revealed her deepest secrets to him?

Yes, her heart was broken, and he could pester her constantly about what she wanted for Christmas, but she knew the truth. She wanted something very badly, and she knew she could not have it.

Oh, sure, she would like *Knight in Shining Armor*, it might distract her from what she *really* wanted for a week or two.

Because what she really wanted, her deepest secret, was that she wanted everything to be the way it had been before her nephew had been crippled, before Kent had let down the family so badly. She hoped, in some secret place, that Kent and Becky would get back together. Despite her mother and father's love dying, despite the treachery of James, despite Kent and Becky's breakup, she still wanted, in her most secret place, to *believe*.

A Christmas reconciliation would be the absolute best, a miracle just like the ones you saw in the Christmas movies. Had she written that down somewhere for prying Michael to see?

"I don't appreciate you being in my office, going through my things," she said tightly.

"No need to act as if it's your underwear drawer." He was watching her intently, narrowly. She wanted to turn around and run from what she saw in his eyes.

He would not rest until he knew the truth about her, the whole truth, things she had probably not even totally admitted to herself.

"It's you," he said suddenly, slowly. "It's you who is in the worst pain."

Her heart stopped. He did know then!

"Because of this," he said. "Holy cow, this stuff is hard to handle."

She could tell by the way he was looking at her he'd unearthed her secret. That despite it all—despite being surrounded by people who cared for her, despite bringing joy into a world too filled with sadness—she barely made it through this season.

Her nephew, Grant, had been hit by a car on Christmas Day.

Michael held up the file, and then she blinked. She saw he didn't really know her secret at all. He'd unearthed the Impossible Dreams file. For a moment, when she thought he knew, had she felt truly sorry, or just a tiny bit relieved, as if her burdens were not going to be so heavy to carry? Because she would not have to be so alone with the impossibility of her fantasy of everything working out somehow, someway.

"Dear Santa," he read out loud, "my brother got shot in the head. He needs his brain back. Love, Geoff."

"Now you know the reason I can barely get through Christmas," she whispered.

It felt like a lie, a terrible lie, even if these children with their impossible dreams had become so linked to her fate.

This was how she was trying to fix everything but in her most honest moments she knew it wasn't working. Still, she was not ready to tell Michael the whole truth. And maybe she never would be. He might think he could do the impossible, but she knew no one could set back the clock.

"Dear Santa," he read the next letter, "My mom diet last yer. Is she in hefen?" He swore under his breath.

"Michael, don't."

He glared at her, read the next one and the next one. "At least Disneyland and sports stars are somewhat possible. What are we going to do about this, Kirsten?" he said.

We?

"Impossible dreams," he said when she was silent. "We can't let those kids think their dreams are impossible."

There was that seductive *we* again.

"One of them asks to go to heaven to see his mommy!" He had to accept that some dreams *were* impossible. That was life.

"Okay, that one's a little tougher."

"And we can't send anyone to Disneyland."

"Why not?" he asked stubbornly.

"Michael, if we did that, word would get around. Just ask Santa and you, too, can be on your way to Disneyland. Next year that's the only request we would get. Even if we could arrange it, just once, it would lead to a thousand other disappointments."

"You've got the weight of the whole world on your shoulders, don't you?"

She hated this—that he was making her think her own impossible dream was not so impossible after all, that he was making her think maybe love was real, after all, even in the face of the fact she'd seen so much evidence that it could fall apart in a blink.

And that's the last thing she wanted to feel. She didn't even want to have a shred of belief that impossible things could happen.

Hope, the most dangerous thing of all.

She'd taken Michael on: told him she knew how he would get through this. She'd invited him into her own little family, her safe place.

Now she was sorry, because it was not feeling quite so safe anymore. He was rattling her. She had wanted to fix his world, but she had not expected hers would be so challenged in the process.

He was making her ache for things she didn't want to believe in: strong arms to hold her in the night, someone to talk to, someone to believe in, someone to share the burden.

He was making her long for things she thought she had wisely given up on: a desire to be safe, protected, loved, looked after, secure. A desire to be able to trust again: the world, men, *herself*.

He was making her thirst for a man who would push away her barriers and make the wild side of her sing. He was making her *want* to taste passion in the form of his lips and his skin against her own, his eyes hot on her.

She tried to remind herself how angry she had been when she'd first walked in and seen he had made himself at home at her desk so that she could push him away.

But looking at the expression on his face as he read those letters, she could summon no anger. How could he always turn everything around? Now she was even more under his spell.

Kirsten could tell by the grim look of absolute determination on Michael Brewster's face that he didn't intend to accept that anything was impossible.

CHAPTER SIX

Eighteen days until Christmas...

"ONE more thing before we lock up," Michael said. "Kirstie, I've got something to show you." He tried for a casual tone, but he knew how his father had felt all those Christmas mornings when he had kept that special Christmas surprise until last. Not that this was her Christmas surprise—he was still working on that—but it was a nice warm-up for it.

"Lock up?" she said. "I don't want to lock up. I want to stand here and marvel at this."

He laughed. "It's nearly midnight."

Still, she walked around the "sleigh" one more time. "It's the best it's ever been," she declared.

A man could puff up like a peacock around that kind of flattery, though the sleigh did look pretty good. When he had first been shown the old sleigh, an old flat deck made over, he'd been appalled. He wasn't even sure how no one had ever been hurt the construction had been so rickety. With lots of enthusiastic help, he'd torn it down to the floorboards and started over. Now it was a work of art—velvet driver's seat for Santa, huge brightly painted boxes to hold the gifts for the kids, carpeted walkways so that the elf, if they ever found such a creature, could get at the gifts.

All the other volunteers had drifted home after a wonderful night of organizing the sleigh. It was really like a float that would be pulled by a truck down the streets on Christmas Eve, making deliveries. They would be setting a new record this year: twelve hundred individually requested gifts, not including the Impossible Dreams file.

Still, for all that he was happy about the sleigh, what he was about to present her with was his greatest accomplishment at the Secret Santa Society to date.

He brought a large box, as yet unwrapped, from where he had set it by the door earlier in the evening. Now he put it in front of her. He stood back as she peeked in.

"What is it?" she asked.

"Impossible Dream Number Twelve, Amanda Watson, age six," he said.

"Disneyland?" she gave him a skeptical look, but as she began to poke through the box the skeptical look melted into the one he waited for, maybe even lived for. The worry line on her brow melted. The lines around her mouth tilted up. The sun came on in eyes that were made to laugh and didn't do it often enough.

"Disneyland," he proclaimed with satisfaction. "Disneyland in a box."

"Look at this wallpaper," she gasped.

It had taken him three days of hunting to find it and the look on her face made every frustrating moment of that search worth it. It was a mural style, King Ludwig's castle in Neuschwanstein, which had inspired the Sleeping Beauty Castle at Disneyland. Then there was bedding—sheets, pillows, a quilt—with all the Disney favorites cavorting on it. Next came huge stuffed toys of the most popular characters.

And last, in the very bottom of the box was the best of all. Michael watched Kirsten's face as she tenderly took out the princess costume: a tie on dress of taffeta and satin and lace, the little bejeweled crown, the clear plastic slippers that a child's imagination would transform to glass.

Her eyes filmed with tears as she clutched the dress. "Oh, Michael," she said. "How can you be so full of surprises? How could you know this? That a little girl would love this?"

"Santa seems to be whispering in my ear," he said, as surprised as her by how inspired he was when it came to these Impossible Dreams tasks.

She sighed. The worried look came back. "It's too much for one child," she said reluctantly. "We'll divide it up. There's enough here for—"

"Over my dead body," he said, firmly.

The worried look disappeared and she laughed. "Oh, Michael! You were swarmed when you picked out this dress weren't you?"

"When I picked out the crown thingie, every woman in that store was smiling at me as if I was the most adorable thing!"

"Tiara," she told him, touching the item in question with a certain reverence only someone of the female persuasion could manage for such a piece of fluff and foolishness.

"—and the whole time I was thinking of Amanda's drawing with the castles and cartoon characters and Cinderella. Focusing on that little girl was the only way I survived the experience. You wouldn't cheat the girl who saved my life, would you?"

"Okay, Michael, you win." He could tell it was a victory

Kirsten was more than pleased to give him. Besides, Amanda getting everything in this box did not mean other children would do without. Not on his watch. Not while he was doing Santa duty.

She laughed again, making every second of torture in that store called "Girlie-Girl" worth it. "I would have loved to have seen you buying this." She waved the dress at him.

"Yeah, you and two dozen other women. I thought I was going to die. Cinderella does not come naturally to me. The next one was easier."

For Impossible Dream Number Three, a request for a personal meeting with a top basketball player, Michael Brewster had been able to cruise the Internet and find a signed picture. After that it had been a quick trip to the store for a team jersey, number twenty-three, and that had been that.

The strangest thing had happened. Michael had thought that the Impossible Dreams file was going to be a heart-breaker, but he had wanted to take the burden off Kirsten. He figured he didn't have much of a heart left to break, anyway.

To his amazement, he loved the Impossible Dream file. Fulfilling those tough requests made him feel alive as he had not felt alive since that day he had been pulled from the water. It was true, some dreams were impossible. He couldn't get Geoff's brother a new brain, he couldn't bring back a mother gone to heaven. But he *could* work with the spirit of Christmas. Geoff's brother was going to get extra remedial therapy. He'd arranged for a local bakery to deliver chocolate chip cookies once a week for a year to the little kid with no mom.

He had come to anticipate the look on Kirsten's face when he crossed another item off the list, showed her his solution. It made him feel ten feet high and bulletproof, more like a man than he had ever felt, even when he was doing the most manly things, pulling crab pots, or swinging a hammer.

"Michael, we should go. It's after midnight."

He knew she was right. The days as they counted down to Christmas did not hold enough hours. Still, he didn't want to leave here, or leave her.

"But that's when all the magic happens," he told her. "I bet if you put on that slipper, it would fit."

She gulped, looked around like a rabbit cornered by the hounds. It was almost as though she hated the fact she loved the way he made her feel.

"No, it wouldn't! I'm afraid I'm destined to be the ugly stepsister."

He wished he could change that about her—the fact that she didn't understand her own understated appeal. But he only knew one way to change it, and that seemed like it would make a complicated situation even more complicated.

So he did what men do. He held open the outside door for her and changed the subject. "I have a pretty good idea for Impossible Dream number six—"

But before he could tell her, she had scooped up a handful of snow and thrown it at him. That playful side of her came out more and more, surprising, delighting.

The snowball fight was on! They chased each other up and down the deserted street in front of the Secret Santa Society office. She had quite an arm for a girl who didn't look as if she had ever played baseball.

Michael spun around and aimed, but before he could let loose with his own snowball, *sploosh*—hers, wet and heavy caught him right in the face.

He wiped the dripping snow away, let loose his own, but

Miss Kirsten Morrison dodged with the expertise of a soldier dodging bullets.

Her laughter rang out through empty streets. A brand-new blanket of thick snow had not yet been churned into mud and slop by passing feet and traffic. The snow transformed the grimness of even this street, made it white and sparkling and magical. Which was what he knew his kiss would do to her.

And hers to him. Transform him. Was he ready?

Each day now, more and more volunteers showed up at the Secret Santa Society.

Each day, he could feel her and him solidifying into more of a team, uniting in their purpose to bring Christmas to these streets that could be so mean.

Reminded of the meanness of the streets, despite the cloak of white they hid under, he realized she was getting a little too far away from his protection, even now. Sometimes, on nights like this, drug addicts and drunks sought refuge in those doorways.

"Hey," he called. "Come back. Truce."

She looked over her shoulder, and he tossed down his already formed snowball, held up his hands in surrender.

Twelve hundred gifts and a swiftly diminishing timeline added up to an almost impossible workload. Kirsten was always the last one at the Secret Santa Society office, and he never left until he was sure she was safe.

Now she came back down the street toward him, hands in her pockets, probably frozen from making snowballs. She tilted her chin up and caught a snowflake on her tongue.

He could tell she was disappointed that he had declared the truce. Where was she getting all the energy from? Like him, she was putting in at least sixteen-hour days.

When she came close to him, he met her halfway, tugged her snowball frozen hands out of her pockets, cupped them between his own and blew his breath on them to warm them.

There was an old Michael who would have never been so gentle. Still, there was enough of the old Michael there to register the look on her face and take advantage of it.

"What do you want for Christmas?" he asked her, in between breaths.

It came to him with the suddenness of being hit by a snowball out of the darkness of night. It hit him—*sploosh*—that he was falling in love with her.

Only the thought did not fill him with terror, and it did not make him run away.

He only contemplated it, feeling a stillness grow inside of him as he blew on her hands and looked into the gray of her eyes that had become so familiar.

"What you're doing right now is pretty good," she said, and then sang in a surprisingly horrible voice, "Merry Christmas to me."

"I'm serious!"

"So am I."

"Come on, Kirsten. Tell me." He realized he wanted her to tell him something that would give him hope that maybe she was ready for this thing that crackled in the air between them to move forward. Trust him with some little piece of herself, even if it was only the fact she wanted the *Little in Love* figurine, *Knight in Shining Armor*.

Nearly, he was discovering, as hard to get his hands on as an elf. The collectors of *Little in Love* were surprisingly mean-spirited when it came to their collections.

Then, partly sad and partly dreaming, she gave in to him.

She said, "One day. We only give them one day. Wouldn't it be great if we could give them more than that?"

"Such as?"

She hesitated, gave him that look that meant she was trying to decide how far to trust him with her secrets, her dreams, her plans.

He was aware he was holding his breath, and when she sighed, he did, too.

"There's a building around the corner for sale. Brick. A tiny little storefront. I think it used to be a candy store. I dream about buying it and turning it into a reading room. A lovely warm space full of sofas and pillows and books, a little snack table with fresh apples and oranges and bananas…simple, silly, impossible."

Her voice faded, she blinked, her voice became business-like. She laughed halfheartedly. "As if I don't have enough to do already." She seemed to realize he still held her hands, and she pulled them away from him.

Michael sensed that she had really given him nothing at all. Why wouldn't she tell him about herself? Why wouldn't she admit she liked *Little in Love?*

He'd teased her about them, and had some fun with the twirpiness of the names. Was it that easy to lose her trust? Maybe she already knew him too well and could sense his distaste for something so melodramatic, romantic, tender. But he *wanted* her to know he was growing—that he could put aside his personal tastes to make another person happy. Bite back his scorn.

"As noble as that is," Michael said drily, "and though I'll be sure to add it to the Impossible Dreams files, don't you want anything for *you?*"

She looked blank.

"You know, a present? Like china? Or a genuine pair of designer shoes?"

"Good grief, Michael, what do you know about china, and shoes?"

"I know that's what girls want," he said stubbornly. His expertise in what girls wanted was relatively new. He knew because he managed to get it out of each volunteer who came through the doors for his own Secret Santa list. Sandra wanted to add a place setting to her china collection. Lulu—as well as the foot bath—dreamed of owning a genuine pair of designer shoes.

"I know what you're doing," she said. "Don't think you're fooling me."

"What?" he said innocently.

"You're making note of what every one of those people tells you they want. I'm beginning to wonder, if Santa did exist, what would he look like? Michael Brewster?"

"You're still not telling me," he said.

"I'm thinking!"

"Well, take your time. Christmas is a whole twenty days away!"

"Eighteen," she corrected him automatically. "No! It's past midnight. Seventeen."

Which meant he was really going to have to make a decision about the offer from that crabby old lady in Georgia who had told him he could have her reserved *Knight in Shining Armor* over her dead body—or for three thousand dollars.

"I don't want you to get me anything. Michael, seeing you—what you bring to all of us—is gift enough. You don't have to get anybody anything else."

It was a thought a man could stay warm in for a long, long time. That he was *enough* without giving anything besides himself. Suddenly, *Knight in Shining Armor* seemed like it would be worth every penny of the ludicrous asking price.

"That was fun tonight," he said, "I really enjoyed myself. I'm not really giving anything to anybody, I'm taking."

She gave him one of those looks: the could-he-possibly-mean-it look.

"We painted wooden candy canes and touched up Santa's seat," she said. "Christmas music played the whole time, and I hate egg nog by about the third sip."

"It was still fun. I liked it when Lulu pretended to be Santa. Her Santa dance should be recorded." He smiled remembering the big woman's surprising grace as she donned the Santa hat, wrapped herself in red velvet from the float and began to dance to the music. Soon everyone had been clapping and the more they clapped the more she swung her hips, until she looked like Santa doing a striptease and everyone was holding their stomachs they had laughed so hard.

He was being returned to life. To laughter. To warmth.

And he was ready.

Kirsten still looked dubious. "You strike me as a guy who has done a lot of things—wild things, outrageous things, really fun things."

"Such as?" Oh, goodie, she was going to blush.

"Such as judging the wet T-shirt contest at the local watering hole. Such as skiing the out-of-bounds area. I bet you've jumped out of airplanes."

"Just once," he said.

"Bungee jumped?"

"Does it count if I was drunk?"

"Only if you were naked."

She'd say these things—as if she was comfortable saying

them—but the blush always gave her away, except he'd noticed lately she seemed to have better control of the blush. Either that or he was losing his touch. He didn't know why she wanted him to think she was a racier, more experienced girl than she was, but it was endlessly entertaining.

"Shoot," he said. "I guess it counts." Ah, sometimes he still had it, after all. Her face turned crimson under the white glare of the streetlight.

"See?" she sputtered. "And now you expect me to believe you thought tonight was fun?"

"What makes you think bungee jumping naked would be fun?" he asked her, and he was serious. What could be less comfortable than that?

"Well, maybe fun is the wrong word. Uninhibited. Carefree. Not caring what people think."

Now there was an interesting insight into her: world's most responsible girl with a secret longing to be wild.

"You let me know if you want to work on those things. I know where they have a great catch-the-greased-pig contest. Only they don't play it with a pig."

"See?" she said. "Building a sleigh float with a bunch of old people and me has got to seem tame after that. Boring."

"Don't forget Lulu," he admonished her. "No one would ever mistake that girl for tame. And she'd probably kill you personally if she knew you put her in the boring category. She's sure excited about the volunteer Christmas party. She's reminded me three times that it is this weekend and that I need a tux."

"I think for a lot of the volunteers it's the only occasion to really dress up that they have all year. They love that it's formal."

He grimaced. "Not my idea of fun." Still, he had dusted off a tux from a friend's wedding.

"So what is your idea of fun?"

He slid her a look. "Girl, don't even go there."

She planted her arms over her chest. "I am going there. Tell me the best thing you ever did for fun."

Hard choices. The time he and his brother had decorated their very cute Grade Ten teacher's thirty-foot pine, top to bottom, with all her underwear? Maybe that hadn't been so fun. His mother had cried when the police showed up on their doorstep.

The Puerto Vallarta all-inclusive—board-surfing, parasailing, girls in bikinis everywhere and an all-you-could-drink bar?

It seemed, in retrospect, fun but mindless. Besides, Brian had broken his leg in Mexico, and their mother had cried again, because of the medical bill.

He decided he wasn't about to tell her a truth he was growing more aware of all the time. The best thing he had ever done was walk through the doors of the Secret Santa Society, into that secret and magical place built by the spirit of Christmas: love and generosity in such massive abundance as to be nearly blinding.

"I just can't figure out what the attraction of us is," she said. "We're not exciting. We're hardly even interesting."

He looked at her and realized she just didn't have any idea at all. His whole life seemed like it had been uninteresting until the exact moment he'd walked through that door into the world Kirsten had made.

All the things he and his brother had gotten into, they all seemed like childish high jinks now. Not that he would take back a moment of it, but something in him was ready to move on. To grow up.

He was not sure if Brian was still around if that would have ever happened. They egged each other on, they fed off each other's energy, they kept each other company. When one of them had gotten a girlfriend, the other one had usually managed to wreck it somehow, always thinking that girl wasn't just right, wasn't good enough.

What would Brian think of Kirsten?

A keeper. He almost heard his brother's voice, his laughter when their mother nagged them to settle down. *Ma, we're looking for keepers, just like you.*

Well, you aren't going to find anything worth keeping in the trashy places you're looking, their mother had shot back, *there's a nice girl at church...*but before she got any further Brian had laughed and gone and picked her up and twirled her around until she was laughing helplessly, too.

He felt that ache when he thought of his brother's laughter. And his mother's. It felt as if it would swamp him, but he looked at Kirsten's eyes, and the emotional sea inside him seemed to calm.

"I used up all my need for excitement," he said slowly, and then he knew he was going to tell her.

That he was ready to speak of this thing, to trust all of himself to her.

"You know that accident I told you about?"

She nodded.

"My family had a crab boat in Alaska. My dad was raised there, we always went back for the two crab seasons, king crab and snow crab. Do you know anything about crab fishing?"

She shook her head.

"It's cold, it's hard, it's dangerous. The Bering Sea is probably the most dangerous water in the world. And still, it's thrilling. Bringing a boat into Dutch Harbor so loaded that if you put one more crab on it, it would capsize, is like winning the lottery. Same adrenaline rush, same reward.

"In April this year, snow crab, we'd already brought our boat in, fully loaded, once. A storm was coming, the season was close to ending. I didn't want to go back out. We'd cashed in a record catch. Over three hundred grand in crabs.

"My dad wasn't greedy. But crab fishing is like gambling. It's a high. And he always had this grab-life-with-both-hands attitude. He and my brother overruled me and my mom. She always came along to cook, to look after her boys.

"One hundred and eighty miles out in the Bering Sea, *The Queen of Treemont*, named after my mom, went down.

"All souls lost," he said. "All souls lost."

The night seemed to have grown quieter. The snow was falling more heavily.

"Weren't you on it?" she finally whispered. "Didn't you go back out?"

"Oh, yeah, I was there. I survived. Thanks to a survival suit, I was pulled out of the water by a rescue chopper after six hours in a storm-tossed sea. But my soul was lost that night as surely as theirs were. They were my soul, Kirsten."

"I understand," she said quietly.

And oddly, he knew she did. So many people claimed to understand, to know what he was going through. But nobody really did.

But when he looked into her eyes, and saw them blurred with tears that were slipping down her cheeks, he knew she understood. Not what it was like to be him.

What it would be like to love him.

He felt driven to continue, to spill all of this thing that had set like an anchor inside of him, dragging him to the bottom.

"I never saw one of them out there in the water that night. I did not have a chance to save them, and had I known they were all gone, I would have let go instead of hanging on. So many days I regret living. I feel rage at them."

It was the first time he'd said that. Instead of making him feel intensely guilty, he felt free. He felt good that he was trusting Kirsten with all of him, even a man who could feel rage at a dead family.

"What would you say to them if you could?" she whispered.

Ah, a chance to tell them one last time, that he loved them. No. He was determined to give Kirsten all of him.

"What would I say? I'd scream at them. How could you go without me? How could you be all together and leave me alone?"

He was done speaking. He felt heavy with it, and yet, relieved in some way, too. He had thought, when he spoke of this, the dam within him would burst and what was behind it would come rushing out and destroy.

But he could feel the dam bursting, and it felt as if it was love pouring out. Years and years of the love of a strong, strong family. He remembered his mother's hand on his brow when he was sick, his father's hand on his backside after they broke Mr. Theodore's front picture window for the third time. He remembered his brother, two years older than him, Brian's hand in his as they made that long walk to Michael's first day of school.

She reached up and kissed him, and he tasted the salt of her own tears. He kissed her back, gently at first, but then all that was within him, he gave to her. Sorrow, anger, joy, memories.

She took a step back from him.

And he was pretty sure neither of them knew if she was ready for anything quite so real and quite so raw as Michael Brewster.

* * *

Kirsten could barely see him through her tears. How could he suffer something like this and still be able to go and buy a little girl who dreamed of Disneyland everything that was needed to keep a dream alive? How could he do that when his own dreams had been so shattered?

He could do it because he was Michael.

Michael who made everyone laugh, and who hated Christmas music, and who danced with Lulu, and who could put together—or wrap—any odd gift that came through that door. Michael who could turn an old wreck of a flat deck into a real Santa's sleigh.

Michael who was challenging her, every single day, to let go of her stranglehold on control, to risk a little of her heart.

He had told her he was unavailable, and she had tried so hard to believe him. But she sensed in this confidence he had shared with her tonight, something new, something changing, something that could not be put back the way it was before once it had changed.

He was a man who would take everything a woman had to give. He was a man who would even take things that she did not have to give.

She knew she was standing on a precipice, right now, in this snowstorm with Michael. His inner storm was calming, she could feel that. But her own felt as if it was just beginning.

"I'm sorry," he whispered against her ear. "I need to go. I want to be alone."

She looked at him and saw his need to be alone was not about her. It was about him. She could see the memories swimming through his eyes, and she knew how he wanted to be with them.

Kirsten was aware she wanted to be alone as much as he did. She needed time to puzzle over the last days, to puzzle over how she was feeling.

She didn't want to be swept away by emotion.

She wanted to *decide* where her life was going, what risks she was ready to take.

So even though she knew the most sensible thing would be for both of them to be alone, she could not look at the starkness in his face and be sensible.

"Are you sure you don't want to go for a coffee?" she asked, but she heard the tentativeness in her own voice.

"Not tonight," he said. "I'm going to take a rain check."

She turned and walked away from him, aware he watched her as she fitted her key into her lock, still protecting her, even as he embraced the storm of his own feelings. She cleared the windshields with the wipers, rather than getting out and brushing them off. She was aware of needing to run away from her own emotion as she spun the car around and drove away from him.

In her rearview mirror, he was a lonely figure being lost in the snow, and yet she felt a thousand times more lost than him. What did it mean that he had confided in her? That he had made himself so vulnerable to her? Could it possibly mean that he might feel more for her than she had ever believed could be possible? Was she worthy of his trust? And was she ready for it?

CHAPTER SEVEN

MICHAEL watched Kirsten drive away, then shoved his hands in his pockets, trudged through the thickening snow toward the car he and his brother had shared so many good times in… tonight he would open the photo albums he had been avoiding. Tonight, he would remember and embrace the love that had been the lifelong gift from his family. He would make a choice to live in that love rather than in the pain of those final moments.

He had shared his deepest, most painful moments and memories with Kirsten. It had felt like a relief to tell her, it had felt as if finally, after months lost in the storm, he had glimpsed safe harbor. In Kirsten, he had glimpsed safe harbor.

And he knew he was going to be cashing in that rain check for a coffee, even though in Kirsten's world, coffee would mean coffee, he knew that. He knew it even though when she had kissed him the message of her lips had been primal. *Live.*

Whether she knew it or not, and she probably didn't, she was inviting him to live again. Fully. And maybe to love, though the truth was he did not know how you would go about loving a girl like Kirsten.

Slowly, came to mind. No fast moves.

And he knew what being alone, so far, had solved for him—absolutely nothing.

He liked the contradictions of her—her eyes promised him safe harbor, and yet something about her also promised a kind of adventure that was brand-new to him.

A new adventure beckoned. And like the best of adventures it terrified, too. And that combination of curiosity and terror made it irresistible to a heart that he recognized was healing…

Fourteen days until Christmas…

"Hey," Michael said, casually, a few days later as they were locking up, "how about that coffee you promised me?"

Ever since he had spilled his guts to her, something in him was more relaxed, more open. Ready.

She didn't like spontaneity, and he smiled at her expression. "At my house?" she asked.

He could clearly see she was doing inventory of her house, deciding if it was tidy enough. He hoped it wasn't. Untidy would tell him a whole lot more about her!

"That sounds good," he said. "I'll just follow you in my car."

Her apartment building was what he expected—a second-floor walk-up in a well-kept brownstone. The front door of her suite opened into a living room that was pure Kirsten—neat and tidy, after all. There was a lace doily on the coffee table, an ugly hand-knitted afghan thrown over a *white* couch. No one who knew the first thing about real men would buy a white sofa.

A book lay open, spine up, on a side table. He caught a glimpse of it—a lady in a low-cut red dress, head thrown back, bosom thrown forward, vampirelike man posed over her neck.

He felt his pulse quicken. Was there a secret side to

Kirsten much bolder than he had ever imagined? It was going to be hard to go *slowly* if he started thinking she had secret desires.

Kirsten saw the direction of his gaze. She scooped up the book as if it was X-rated underwear, and put it behind her back.

"Is that your book club selection?" he asked innocently.

Just to remind him who she *really* was, she blushed her pure-as-the-driven-snow blush. "No. Lulu gave it to me. Insisted I read it. Her favorite book. It's not to my taste."

"It looked like you were halfway through it," he pointed out.

"In case Lulu asks me!"

"Oh, of course. Maybe I should have a look at it, too. Just to give me more things to talk to Lulu about."

Kirsten glared at him, pointed to the couch. "Have a seat," she ordered. "I'll go make us coffee."

She marched out of the room, the offensive but half-read book clutched to her bosom.

Michael suppressed a grin and looked around. He suspected she had never had a man in this apartment. It had been an act of trust for her to invite him here, and he probably did not deserve it. He had never been in a woman's apartment at this time of night for *just coffee* in his life. The fact of the matter was Kirsten was going to require him to be a better man.

Her couch looked tiny and frail, confirmation that no one over a hundred and fifty pounds had ever sat on it. Better not to sit.

Michael prowled her small living room, trying to get a glimpse of who she was. But aside from that book, the room was predictable.

There was a feeling of something missing, and he realized

what it was: there were no photos. His own house, decorated by his mother, had school pictures of him and his brother from age six on up, on every available wall. Family photos, awards, souvenirs from trips, his mother had seen wall space as a personal challenge. It had to be filled, most of it with mementos of her sons, her husband, her life.

Kirsten had a few generic prints, an oak tree with the sun setting behind it, a beach scene with an empty boat. No family photos. A dining room that looked as if it was never used adjoined the living room and he wandered in. A huge glass china cabinet, darkened, dominated the back wall. He went to it, touched a switch, and the case lit up, showcasing her *Little in Love* collection. It was ghastly and he turned the light back off hastily and retreated back into the living room. He realized what else was missing.

No Christmas tree. No lights. No wreaths. No candles. No candies. No wrapping paper. No ribbons.

"Do you want regular or decaf?"

He heard her clanking around in the kitchen and went through the door she had gone through, leaned against the jamb and watched her. The kitchen was tiny, but it was still a moment before she realized he was watching her. It made her nervous, making him think, again, she hadn't done much entertaining of the opposite sex in her little apartment.

For some reason that pleased him inordinately, even as it served as a reminder. *Best behavior, Brewster.* Which meant no suggesting a glass of wine instead of coffee.

"Decaf."

She spooned grounds into the tiniest coffee machine he had ever seen. Nope, she didn't do much in the way of entertaining. And certainly not morning-after entertaining, though he'd known that even before he'd seen the dead giveaway of the coffee-for-one maker.

Uncomfortable with his scrutiny, she spilled the cream, which she was putting into a dainty glass cream holder. The pink had not receded from her cheeks from his discovery of her reading material and now it darkened.

"Not much in the way of Christmas spirit in this place, Ms. Santa." He looked around her tiny kitchen. No sign of Christmas in this room, either, but at least it was cozy and used, spices lined up neatly on top of the stove, a café style table with this morning's newspaper open on it under a window with bright yellow-checked curtains.

"The elf was supposed to come and decorate," she told him, concentrating furiously on the cream, which was evading her nervous efforts to wipe it up. "But as you well know, no elf."

He took pity on her when it looked as if she was going to knock over another teacup, took the rag from her hand and wiped up cream.

"Oh!" The blush deepened when he accidentally touched her hand, and let his knuckle rest against her forefinger for a breath, a second, a blink.

Strange, he'd had moments with women that would have made that one seem downright laughable in the sexy department.

And yet it wasn't. His knuckle brushing her finger, the sudden heat in her eyes that put the lady in the red dress on the cover of that book to shame, made blood that had been running way too cold through his veins heat. He could suddenly feel the beat of his own heart and see her own pulse going crazy in the hollow of her throat.

Slowly, he reminded himself, but then was amazed how much discipline it took to move away from her. She looked nonplused when he rinsed out the dishcloth, put it in the sink, then took off his jacket, hung it on the back of a chair, sat at her tiny kitchen table.

She looked down at the tray she was getting ready. "I was going to bring this into the living room."

"I'm a kitchen table kind of guy," he said.

"I don't know what that means."

"Nothing sexual," he told her, "unfortunately."

As he had hoped, she went scarlet. What he wasn't prepared to deal with was his own sudden image of her. And him. And that kitchen table. Which did not look nearly sturdy enough to handle that kind of activity.

Look at her cheeks, man! She can't handle that kind of activity, either! Yet. And that one tiny word, *yet,* almost swamped the discipline he was trying so hard to achieve.

"Do you have a deck of cards?" He was aware his voice was faintly hoarse.

"Cards," she repeated, and then she scowled at the tray she'd been making, obviously flustered. Apparently she thought they were going to sit in her parlor with their pinkies out trying to think of things to say to one another. "Cards?"

"Playing cards. I'll teach you how to play Ninety-Nine."

She looked at him suspiciously. "And is that something sexual?"

It delighted him that she was always trying to throw out these tentatively racy lines, as if she talked about sex at one in the morning in her kitchen all the time, when she didn't have a hope of pulling it off.

And at the same time, her words had the same effect on him as his knuckle brushing her forefinger. The tension in the room was becoming supercharged.

He contemplated that with amazement. Neither of them even had their clothes off! Not even a button undone at her prim little throat. It wasn't even likely to happen! *Yet.* He felt as if he'd just run the Boston Marathon, his heart was beating so hard.

"No," he said, "Unfortunately." He warned himself not to play with fire, but who could resist playing with fire? "But if you'd prefer a little poker for clothing items, I'm game."

She stared at him. She licked her lips. He really wished she wouldn't do that. Then she glanced at the door. Contemplating running? Or going and changing into something more comfortable?

Slowly, he reminded himself sternly.

He laughed, hoping she wouldn't hear the uneasiness, the temptation, the wickedness. "I'm kidding you."

Ah, Kirsten. Always could be counted on to surprise. Because he had thought she would look relieved. Instead she looked indignant—as if she wasn't good enough to play strip poker. He looked at the button at her throat. One hand, he thought. Just to get that button undone. He gave himself a mental slap. *Don't even go there, buster.*

This was a good girl. The kind his mother had always dreamed of for him. *Be worthy.*

"At Christmas, my family sat around the kitchen table and played cards." And not any evil varieties, either, he reminded himself. "Sometimes about fifty of us, sometimes just my brother, my mom and dad and me."

It was an opening for her to say what her family traditions were at Christmas, but she was now carrying the coffee tray, tongue caught between her teeth as though her life depended on not spilling one more drop of cream. She set the things on the table, whirled away from him, pawed through a drawer, came out with a deck of cards looking amazed and pleased with herself that she possessed such a thing.

It was a souvenir deck, the wrapper not even off. He opened the cards, shuffled, while she poured coffee and then sat down. He was not unaware that Miss Pure-as-the-driven-snow kept glancing at his hands. She had definitely felt that tingle when they had touched, too.

She sat down, he dealt the cards, explained the values of each and the game to her. She caught on quickly, began to loosen up, just as he had hoped she would. He was able to get his mind out of the gutter, which he had hoped he would. By the third hand she was laughing, and he was focusing on the game.

"Don't even try to cheat," he warned her.

"I would never cheat!"

No, probably not. "My dad cheated," he said, smiling remembering. "He was so competitive. He literally would cheat to win. A full-grown man, successful, mostly mature, could not stand to be beaten at cards."

"That's adorable."

"Yeah. My brother, on the other hand, always had to play for something—quarters if my mom was around, anything else if she wasn't."

"Such as?"

"Golf tees, chocolate-covered raisins, his ball cap collection. We played for condoms on more than one occasion."

Had he deliberately made her blush? Of course! But the price was his mind was right back in the gutter, right on the top button of her blouse. *Think of your mother!*

"And my mom," he said, with a shake of his head, pretending he didn't even notice Kirsten was choking on her coffee. "Hopeless at cards. Too busy making sure the chip bowl was full and the coffee topped up to concentrate. She never got the face cards right. Always played a Queen for a Jack. Nobody ever told her, though, because she'd get so excited when she thought she was going to win."

It was the first time remembering them had been like this: like entering their embrace, feeling the love that had been their lifelong gift. He knew he was making a choice, right then, right there, to live in the love rather than in the pain of those final moments. He knew he was making the choice deliberately, and he knew he was making it so that he would be worthy of loving again.

"Want to see their pictures?" he asked.

"Oh, yes."

He took out his wallet, realized he had not looked at these particular pictures for a long time. He passed her the one of Brian.

"He looks just like you," Kirsten said, and then touched the picture with gentle fingertips, as though she could touch his brother's face.

"If he looks just like me, how come he always got the girls?"

"I don't believe you."

He grinned, passed her the picture of his mom.

"Oh, Michael, I know *exactly* what she was like. Chocolate chip cookies and homemade cold remedies. Lots of scolding, too, I bet."

"My right earlobe is still longer than my left one from her pulling it so frequently. See?"

Kirsten studied his earlobe. "I can clearly see."

Unfortunately it was just like touching her hand, just like even *thinking* of her and that kitchen table, or her and a couple of hands of poker. The air was suddenly charged, as if she was nibbling on his ear, instead of just looking at it.

He looked back at his wallet, remembered, with effort, what he was doing. "And this is my dad."

"Handsome, hmm? Runs in your family."

He'd always known that. That he was good-looking, and that women usually thought so. Still, hearing it from her, he could feel himself puffing up dangerously.

If she looked at his ear again, there was no telling what might happen next!

But she didn't. She looked at the pictures for a long time, studied them, passed them back. "I'm sorry I'll never meet them."

"Yeah," he said, relieved by the change in mood. "Me, too." Then he put the pictures away and dealt another hand of cards. He taught her how to shuffle, but she bent the cards so badly while she was learning that it was like playing with a marked deck.

An ideal time to up the ante. "Want to play for something?" he asked.

"Like what?"

Kisses. "I have a dirty mind. You think of something."

The adorable flustered look, the blush and then, as if she had a few ideas she didn't want him to know about, either, she said, with way too much enthusiasm, "Tea!"

He felt a sigh within himself. *Tea.* That was the kind of girl he was dealing with. Totally new. And yet refreshing, too.

"I'll cover your tea with a—" She was holding her breath, terrified he'd say condom. "A quarter," he said. "I only have about two bucks worth, so take it easy on me."

An hour later he found himself in possession of a mountain of bright individually wrapped tea bags with names like Mango Madness, Blueberry Beauty, Peach Passion.

And he resigned himself to the fact he'd succeeded. He'd been a gentleman. The only passion he was going to see tonight was the peach-tea-bag variety.

He stretched, reached for his jacket, stuffed the pockets full of tea bags. "I've got to go, Kirsten. Big day tomorrow. Impossible Dream Number 25, an igloo for Ishmael."

She walked him to the door, the ease that had developed during the card game evaporated from her. At the door she started looking everywhere but at him. He made it easy for her. He reached down, took her chin and kissed her lightly on her mouth.

It was just like touching her hand, only a hundred times worse. It made him *want* to taste her, to touch her, to know her as completely as a man can know a woman.

"Good night," he said, and bolted out the door.

It wasn't until he was wiping yet more snow off his vehicle that he realized something troubling about the evening: he had given her everything.

And she had given him nothing in return. He didn't know one thing about her family, or their traditions. He still didn't know what she wanted for Christmas. He turned and looked at her window. She was watching him, and even though it embarrassed her that she'd been caught, she waved.

He lifted his hand and waved back. But he wondered, why couldn't she tell him the truth? Why was it she could make Christmas so special for everyone else, all the while she couldn't accept one single thing for herself?

Kirsten watched until he drove away. Had she, somewhere in her heart, hoped for a moment like the ones they had just shared?

Well, not exactly like that. Hadn't she hoped, that despite her determination to make decisions rationally, that he would force her hand, sweep her away? That he would come, like this, in the night, only masterful, take her in his arms, kiss her until she couldn't breathe? Or think?

Shut off her mind, a mind that was frightened, and scarred and that demanded complete safety and security.

Instead he had played cards with her, told her about his family, gone slowly with her, as if she was a teenager on her first date. Or maybe even worse than that. Maybe Michael was relegating her to the dreaded position of *friend*.

But whatever he was doing, Michael Brewster had not treated her like a mature woman. Or at least not the way she expected he would treat a mature woman. Even a woman as wary of love, *feelings,* as she was didn't want a man like Michael treating her like his best buddy.

Though she was far from knowing what she did want from their relationship, she knew it wasn't that!

And she knew what she was going to do about it: what any red-blooded all-American girl would do about it. She was going shopping.

Michael Brewster was going to take one look at her at the volunteer party and know she was as grown-up as he was. She thought of the way his lips had tasted, and how they made her feel, the way her heart had leaped at the merest brush of his hand. And she wondered if it was sensible for a girl like her to be playing with a force like that. And for once in her life she didn't want to be sensible!

She had felt something shift in him that night when he had told her about his family and their terrible accident. There was a new warmth in him, an openness. It made him even more attractive than before—which underscored her own doubts about her suitability for him.

But could she not, just like Cinderella, have her one night, her one moment, before she had to live with the reality, again, that she did not trust love?

Kirsten found exactly the dress for a girl determined to have her one night as Cinderella.

Right in the middle of the store, on a raised platform, with a spotlight shining on it was a dress.

No, not really a dress, but a dream.

Red, it swept to the floor, in a shimmering wave of color. The line of it was intensely simple: form-fitting, a plunging bodice, a nonexistent back, a skirt that began to subtly flare out at the hip, until where it touched the floor it was a swirl of pure cranberry sensuality.

Kirsten knew as soon as she saw it that she had to have it. She could be transformed from frumpy to glamorous in one night, a Cinderella story, from ordinary girl to princess with the wave of, well, a magic credit card.

This was the kind of dress that opened a man's eyes, and that took a woman from being relegated to the dreaded friend position to something quite different.

A dress like this invited a woman to play with her deepest secrets, to reveal her sexiest self. A dress like this would make a man absolutely helpless.

When she put it on, the dress did everything Kirsten had known it would and more. By the time she had shoes and some simple jewelry to go with it, she was over her whole Christmas budget by three hundred dollars.

And she simply did not care. The dress banished Kirsten-the-practical, Kirsten-pure-as-the-driven-snow, Kirsten-as-Ms.-Santa. The dress welcomed a different Kirsten: bold, sensuous, mature, *irresistible*.

CHAPTER EIGHT

Ten days until Christmas...

MICHAEL had not worn the tux since his friend Brad's wedding, and now that he was wearing it he felt distinctly stupid.

That's where love got you, he thought. Dressed in a monkey suit, at the florist's picking up a corsage. Tonight was the volunteer Christmas party, held in one of the smaller ballrooms of the very classy Treemont Hotel. The hotel donated the entire affair to the hardworking volunteers of the Secret Santa Society.

There certainly wouldn't be room at their office to have a party. Every space, floor to ceiling, was now stuffed with gifts. It was giving Michael a headache trying to think how they were going to get all that stuff on the sleigh.

And that wasn't all that was giving him a headache. Kirsten was mystifying. He'd told her his entire life story, and he felt as if he knew less about her every day. She didn't open up about anything, not even with hints. Was it possible she didn't feel as strongly about him as he did about her? Sheesh, he'd even managed to get her *Knight in Shining Armor* for Christmas.

That thought, that she might not care about him to the

same extent he cared about her, clouded his mind as he drove up to her apartment.

But when he saw her, his doubt fled.

A woman did not dress like this for a man she did not care about! He stood staring at the woman who had opened the door to him, stunned.

It was not the Kirsten he knew from the Secret Santa Society, adorably unaware of her own attractions, or blissfully hiding them under a sweatshirt six sizes too large.

No, this Kirsten was gorgeous, her hair upswept, makeup making her eyes look huge, her cheekbones look glorious and her mouth look absolutely irresistible.

Little diamond gumdrops drew his eyes to her ears, and then the creamy, lovely lines of her throat, the dipping sensuality of the neckline of that dress. The dress hugged her gorgeous feminine lines—more gorgeous than he could have guessed, and he had done plenty of guessing. More gorgeous than he had assumed even when he had caught glimpses of her taut tummy, her fine long legs.

He felt like a schoolboy as he stood there gawking at her. "You look stunning," he finally said. "Breathtaking. Ohmygod gorgeous!"

"Stop it," she said, and when she blushed he was relieved to see his old Kirsten right there, just below that extremely sophisticated surface.

"If you want a guy to stop it, you don't wear that," he teased her. "Were you inspired by that book Lulu lent you?"

That was better! He could get her cheeks to match that dress if he worked on it.

He had not told her about the corsage, but the florist had suggested white if he didn't know the color of her dress.

Now, he found himself fumbling with the box. Finally he had the corsage in his hand and was glaring at the bodice of the dress.

"Oh, boy," he muttered. "Awkward moment."

She laughed, her blush deepened. He took the corsage and the pin, and touched the fabric of that dress which was slippery and soft and sensual. He could feel the soft swell of her breast, even though he was trying desperately not to. If he got any hotter, he was going to have to ask for a pitcher of ice water before they left!

Finally he stepped back. The corsage was crooked, but be damned if he was going to try to fix it. At the moment, he didn't even want to go to the party. He wanted to persuade her to go back in the apartment, turn the lights down low, put on some slow soft music, drink some wine and let what happened happen.

"Thank you," she said. "I've never had a corsage before."

"What? You must have had one for the prom."

"No. I didn't go."

And suddenly, he didn't want a night in the apartment with her. Well, he did, but he wanted something more. He wanted her to have all the things she hadn't had before. It felt as if it was his personal mission tonight to make up for every fickle, shallow, superficial guy who had ever overlooked a girl like her, who had ever hurt a girl like her.

He extended his arm to her, walked her out to the car, opened the door for her, helped her get all that skirt into a very small space.

The Christmas party was surprisingly fun. There was a great dinner. Games. The hilarious election of Lulu as this year's Santa Claus.

And then there was dancing. Everyone wanted to dance

with Kirsten, but Michael finally put his foot down and had her to himself.

"Your dancing has improved," she told him when he pulled her in close. It hadn't really. He just was dancing the way he liked to dance, holding her in close to him, so he could feel the beat of her heart through the decided flimsy fabric of that dress.

They slow danced under the mistletoe. Had she guided him over here, little minx?

But he'd been fighting temptation for as long as a man could be expected to fight it. Besides, Lulu had told him she had never lent Kirsten a book, so he had to surmise she liked the kind of thing that had been depicted on that cover—or was at least curious about it.

He took her lips, and explored them. He didn't know if the music stopped or if they had stopped, but she twined her arms around his neck and kissed him back.

And she kissed back like a lady who knew exactly what a red dress did to a man.

"You're scaring the hell out of this poor carpenter and fisherman," he said against her ear.

"Why?"

"You look exactly like a woman who is waiting for a knight in shining armor. A princess waiting for a prince."

"And there's something wrong with that?"

"I'm just an ordinary guy, Kirstie," he said quietly. "I'm nobody's fantasy."

He didn't want to scare her off but he wanted it to always be about the truth, and straight from the heart.

"I hate this suit. The tie is choking me."

She found the tie, undid it briskly and dropped it on the floor. He smiled, shook his head, continued: "I can be counted on to walk across a freshly swept floor with mud on my boots, I swear too much, I'm insensitive as hell. I own two pairs of jeans, one for work and one for dress-up and a leather jacket I never intend to part with. I'm not much of a dancer and have been known to drop a girl during that all important dip.

"On the other hand," he said, interpreting her speechlessness as an invitation to go on, "when I am thoughtful, I really mean it. I can cook mean buffalo wings. I know how to do my own laundry and I don't expect anyone else to do it for me."

She nodded sagely. "Why are you telling me this?"

He looked into the clear of her eyes, at the tiny smile on her lips, and thought *it's time*. Time to declare himself. Time to see if she felt anything the same way.

And if she did? Could he trust himself when he took her home in that red dress?

"It's time," crackled over the loudspeaker.

Startled, he thought someone was reading his mind, but then he saw Mr. Temple, resplendent in an electric-blue tuxedo that must have dated to the disco days had taken the stage.

"Kirsten, can you come on up here?"

Kirsten gave Michael a regretful look, wrinkled her nose, kissed his hand and then let it go.

She joined Mr. Temple on the stage, and acted surprised and tearful when she was presented with *A Little Puppy Love*.

Mr. Temple gave a speech. "I personally want to thank you for being an inspiration to all of us, Kirsten. To me it is amazing how you turned your personal tragedy into such a remarkable service to this city. I thank you, and I know I speak for all of us, for turning an event that could have made many of us feel hate, into an opportunity to love."

Amidst the wild cheering, Michael felt something in him

go very still. What tragedy? He knew Kirsten held back from him, but he had thought it was her natural reserve. Why had she allowed him to tell her everything and not once offered anything back? What he felt was deeper than frustration, closer to betrayal.

Tonight, he had been about to offer her his biggest secret. Suddenly he felt glad he had not. He had been about to trust her with everything, and he was not sure she had ever trusted him at all.

Kirsten kept casting glances at Michael as he drove them home. He looked absolutely astonishing in his tux, even better now that the tie was off and he opened the buttons at the throat.

But for the last part of the evening he had gone very quiet. Was it that kiss that had shaken him?

It certainly had her! Shaken her and filled her with the most delicious sense of anticipation. The dress had been worth every cent! No man had ever looked at her the way Michael had looked at her tonight, and the feelings in her were intoxicating.

But as she glanced at his face, now at a stopped light, she wondered if she had missed something.

Michael didn't look as if he was anticipating anything. He looked remote, and faintly grim.

"Is everything all right?" she asked him.

And when his only answer was a shrug, she knew it wasn't. He parked in front of her apartment, helped her from the car, lifted her new collectible from the trunk. The look on his face grew even grimmer.

She put her key in the door, went in, he followed her and set *Puppy Love* on the coffee table.

Once, she would not have been able to keep herself away

from her new figurine, but her interest in it was stopped cold by the look on his face when he turned and looked at her. He folded his arms across his chest, almost as if he was trying to protect his heart from her.

"What's wrong?"

"What tragedy?" he asked quietly.

"They shouldn't have mentioned that."

"No, maybe not. Maybe you should have. You've sucked my entire life story out of me, and not trusted me with one thing about yourself. I thought we were friends."

Sucked? Plus, *I thought we were friends.*

She thought of the last few weeks, and the word friend did not seem strong enough to describe what was going on between them. She felt disappointed by it. She'd laughed with him. Plotted with him how to make dreams come true. Danced with him. Kissed him. Heard his secrets. Friends? And yet she knew he was right. She had held back from him, afraid to take those final steps of trust that loving a man like him would demand from her.

"You know my every damn secret," he said, his voice a growl, "I gave you my soul. And I don't know the first thing about you."

"I keep trying to tell you I'm boring!" she defended herself desperately, but she knew there was no defense. He had been fearless. She had been fearful. Knowing she was in the wrong should have humbled her, but it made her feel prickly, and on edge, trapped in a corner.

"You won't even tell me that you want that stupid figurine for Christmas. *Knight in Shining Armor.*"

He wanted her to risk? She risked. "Because you'd think it was stupid. Don't think I didn't see the look on your face when you carried in *Puppy Love*. And what's the point of telling anyone you want something you can't have? *Knight in Shining Armor* likely sold out within hours of being offered. And not for a price anyone I know could pay. How do you know that, anyway? That I wanted it?"

"You practically wore the print off that page in your catalog. You know the one? You keep it hidden in your top drawer of your desk."

"You were spying on me!"

"Maybe you have to spy on people who don't trust you enough to tell you anything. Not one little thing. Everything as hidden as that damned catalog." He didn't look even a little bit contrite. He glared at her, then kicked off his shoes without invitation. She thought maybe he was going to go flop down on her couch—which suddenly seemed small and foolishly feminine—and they were going to talk this out.

Instead he marched right to her display cabinet. He opened the door.

"Don't touch that," she said when he picked up *First Little Kiss*.

"You scared I'll break it, Kirstie?" he asked.

She had the strangest feeling he wasn't talking about her figurine at all, but about her heart. "Yes," she whispered, "I'm afraid you'll break it."

He flipped it over and inspected the bottom. "Hand-painted in India," he said cynically. "Probably by some poor little kid in rags, chained to a table."

"Stop it!" she said, feeling the blood drain from her face. "You'll wreck it!"

"You know what? That's what reality does. It wrecks fantasy. But you know what else? Sometimes reality is better."

"No, it's not!" Her voice sounded shrieky. "On Christmas Day, four years ago," she said, "my nephew was hit by a car. He was six at the time. He's in a wheelchair now. He was hit by an eleven-year-old boy who stole a car because he was filled with helpless rage because, not only didn't Santa come to his house, his little sister was crying. They didn't even have milk!

"You want to know everything about me? That's why I started all this. That's why I became the Secret Santa Society. Because I don't ever want any kid in Treemont to ever do what he did again! So, see? That's what I want. For no kid ever to wake up without presents again. That's the reality I want."

He knew it wasn't the total truth; she could tell he knew by the look in his eyes, deep and piercing.

"Tell me the rest," he said. He put down the figurine and came back to her. She had the feeling he wanted to shake her but restrained himself by folding his arms over a chest that struck her as being enormously masculine. "That's not the reality you want. Tell me the rest."

Right from the beginning she had known this: that he was the most dangerous man because he would not ever settle for what a person wanted to give—he wanted everything or nothing at all.

She took a deep breath. "Okay. What I really want is for my life to be what it was before, and it can't be, okay? It can't be!"

"What changed?" he said. Oh! She'd told him enough. She didn't want to tell him any more.

But that was the problem: a man like this was never going to accept just what you wanted to give him. He was never going to accept anything less than all of you, even if some of that was not what you wanted anyone to see. Even if some of that was fear-filled and afraid and hateful.

"My sister and my nephew moved to Arizona," she said stiffly. "It's easier to get a wheelchair around there with no snow to contend with six months of the year."

He looked at her closely. She was not sure she had ever felt someone so close to reading her soul.

"They're not even coming back for Christmas this year!"

He had lost so much, and she was whining about her life? She felt ashamed.

"Anyway." She shrugged, "Life goes on—"

"No!" he snapped. "There's more. What changed?"

She refused to cry. She refused to remember the days and years before that accident, moments that had played out so much like Harriet and Smedley. Moments that shone with love and laughter.

"My parents got divorced as soon as I finished high school." She felt ashamed for digging up this old history, but here was the absolute truth, maybe more truth than she had ever admitted, even to herself. "And then in college I started dating a guy who every girl in the school had a secret crush on. He sweet talked me, and made my head swim, and I was not sensible the way I usually am. I didn't sleep, I didn't eat. I just thought of him."

"Ah, James."

It hurt that he remembered. It hurt because it meant he listened to her, and cared about her and hadn't believed her for a minute when she'd told him she'd gotten over all this long ago.

"It was a ridiculously short romance. Six weeks." Long enough for a girl as sensitive and as hopelessly romantic as she had been to be hurt irrevocably. "I was so infatuated, I would have done just about anything for him. Almost anything. He wanted me to cheat on his math exam so he could stay on the football team."

"Well, you're lucky that's all he wanted," Michael said without an ounce of sympathy.

"And into all that, my sister Becky started dating a really great guy named Kent Baker. And it made me believe good things could happen all over again. They got married in a fairy-tale ceremony. They e-mailed me pictures from their honeymoon. I remember how joy-filled they were that a baby was on the way. I remember them buying their first house. I actually started to think, well, maybe good things can happen after all."

She jerked herself away from the warmth of those memories, looked Michael in the eye.

"My sister and her husband split up after Grant's accident," she finally said, trying not to cry. "He had an affair. When she needed him most, the bastard had an affair. Okay?"

He mulled it over, and apparently decided it wasn't okay. It wasn't enough. He wasn't stopping until he had stripped her to her soul. "No. What changed in *you?*"

She stared at him. Then she sighed, and let out her deepest truth and her deepest secret. "Once I believed in love. Now I don't. That's what changed. In me."

And then she knew the truth of why she had held back from him. Because to be with a man like this she would have to let go of her fears, revise her belief system, *change.* Change a way of being in the world that was safe for her, risk-free.

Finally he looked satisfied that she had given him the full truth.

"A month ago," he said quietly, "Mr. Theodore gave me an impossible assignment. He told me to find someone in more pain than I was in, and help them.

"I didn't believe anyone could be in more pain than me.

But now I see that's not true. You see, Kirsten, I *want* what I had before. I want a family, and a home and everything that means. It doesn't mean a stupid fantasy like Harriet and Meddlesome over there.

"It means burnt toast, and fighting over what channel to watch. It means deciding together what to name the baby, and what color to paint the bedroom, then painting it again when you hate it. It means working together, and falling apart, and then working to come together again. It means two people dancing when no one else is around to watch. It means planting trees, and building swing sets, and kissing bruises and going on vacation in a too-small van with a dog who stinks and a tent that leaks. It's about knowing, no matter what happens, you're never ever alone.

"I lost them. I lost my whole family. But I never lost my belief in love. That's the gift they've left with me. That's what I've come to know. I believe that love is the best damn thing— the only thing—worth having in this world."

Slowly he looked at her and shook his head. "And you," he said softly, "you think it's the worst."

"You said," she accused him through tears, "that you weren't available."

"Then I stopped running and found out that I *need* the very thing you are running away from."

"Why are you telling me this?"

"Why do you think, Kirsten?"

She wanted him to spell it out. She wanted him to say that he loved her. But how could he take such a risk, when she had risked nothing for him? Not her heart's secrets.

"And just for the record," he said, "I don't condone what your brother-in-law did, but I understand it."

"You do?" She was glad he said that. Why, she'd been on the brink of loving him! But to understand *that*. She felt fury and indignation sputter to life within her. They felt better, more powerful, than softness and vulnerability. It felt as if he was giving her the excuse she needed to retreat to her safe world.

"Men aren't like Mr. Meddlesome over there," Michael said. "When they feel helpless, sad, destroyed, they'll do anything—absolutely anything—to alter how they are feeling. And they won't always behave well."

"That would explain why I like Mr. Meddlesome—oh! Smedley better."

"They might behave badly, unless they have a soft place to fall. A place they can lay their head where they don't have to be strong, or fix everything. You want your brother-in-law to be the criminal, but maybe your sister wasn't there for him, either."

"Get out!" she said. How dare he delve into the dynamics of her family? How dare he strip her to her soul when she wasn't ready? How much easier to yell at him than to consider what he had to say.

Unfortunately he didn't even look offended. He looked as if he was happy to leave!

"I feel sorry for you," he said, and then he turned and left, closed the door quietly.

That was so different from the declaration of love that she had hoped for when she opened her door to him tonight that she burst into tears. She felt stunned and angry and hurt and helpless. A man who had lost everything *pitied* her.

But through the storm of feelings, a truth shone, the light piercing. Michael had spoken the truth and only the truth. She was in much more pain than he was. Because she had lost her faith in love.

But in the emptiness where he had just stood, she felt a horrible chill. The chill of the loveless way she had chosen to be in the world. Safe, yes, but colorless, cold, empty. She was not really alive at all. Just breathing. Michael was demanding something of her. That she become more than she had ever been willing to be before, that she expose her heart even though there might be arrows aimed at it. To be worthy of him, she would have to live with the kind of courage he had demonstrated.

"I'm not ready," she said out loud, huffily.

But a different voice, quiet, still, calm, deep within her, said *yes, you are*.

CHAPTER NINE

Nine days until Christmas…

MICHAEL pulled up in front of the building around the corner from the Secret Santa Society. The real-estate agent hadn't arrived yet, and Michael waited in his car, mulled over his argument with Kirsten last night.

Fairly satisfactory as far as a first fight went, though he still felt regret that he hadn't been able to get her riled up enough to throw a *Little Love* at him.

When his mother and father had fought, the air had crackled with their passion. A few days cooling off period, then his father begged forgiveness, bought roses, and then they were more in love than ever. People said not to fight in front of kids, but Michael wasn't sure he agreed. His parents' occasional yelling match had taught him love was not fragile. That relationships contained conflict. It was dealt with and then life went on.

He looked at his watch. He probably had time to pop in and see her before the real-estate agent showed up.

He left his car, dashed across the street, horns honking at him, and around the corner. Kirsten was in her office. She slammed her favorite *Little* catalog into her top desk drawer, laced her hands together on top of her desk and looked at him primly.

Her eyes were suspiciously red.

"Yes?" she said.

"Are you okay?" he asked.

"Of course. Fine. Why wouldn't I be?"

He felt as if now would be a good time to lean over that desk and kiss the living daylights out of her, but apparently he had to try to be a bit tamer with her. She was a book club kind of girl, not a woman who could hold her own on a crab boat.

"A job's come up this morning. It's important. That's why I haven't been around."

"You haven't?" she said, feigning surprise.

"It's not because you ordered me out of your house. I'm not that easy to get rid of."

"You're not?" she whispered. And then said quickly, "All right. Thanks. For letting me know. Goodbye."

"It's not goodbye," he said, trying to be patient with her.

"I'm not wounded," she said with grave dignity. "I don't need your pity."

Oh, yeah. His parting words last night. He felt sorry for her. Her eyes shifted away from his. If he was not mistaken, she was looking longingly at the drawer her catalog was in.

He sighed. She was a difficult, complicated woman. Of all the women on the face of the earth, why had his heart picked her? Because she was a difficult, complicated woman. Because she was endlessly fascinating. Because even though she had been hurt, she was still trying so hard to make the world a better place.

She wasn't ordinary. She wasn't superficial. She was a

spring coming from deep, deep in the ground, and once a man had tasted that kind of water, he lost his taste for anything else.

"Look, Kirsten—"

She looked at him, her eyes carefully blank, a horrible phony smile on her face. Here was the thing. She was a book club kind of woman. He, a rough-and-tumble guy who had made his living with his hands, not his head, was never going to be able to find the right words to talk her in or out of anything she had decided to believe. He wanted to tell her to trust him, but that was one of the things she had lost when her nephew got hit, when the world as she knew it had crumbled. She had lost her ability to trust. She *chose* which words she wanted to believe, and she had decided to believe he felt sorry for her.

"It's really hard to feel sorry for somebody that you want to strangle," he said, and moved across the floor toward her. She had no place to go. Her chair was already back against the wall of her tiny space.

He leaned over her desk, put his palms flat down on top of it. She protectively covered her throat, which only made him more annoyed. She really thought he was going to strangle her?

Instead he took advantage of the fact she was defending the wrong part of her anatomy, and took her lips with his own

He wanted to ravage her. To shock her out of her primness. But her lips were sweet, and after just a moment's hesitation, they answered his, soft, giving, supple.

It was not the kiss he thought he craved, a kiss of heat and passion and primal need. Just a gentle kiss that told him, *when you least expected it, you found the other half of your soul.* His kiss told her, *trust me, believe in me.*

And her answer, whether she wanted it to or not, said that she would at least try.

He stepped back from her. "I've got to go."

She nodded.

"By the way," he said. "Did I tell you I've thought it over? I'm available now."

"I'll be sure and post that on the bulletin board," she said.

The urge to strangle her came back. If he had time, he'd straighten her out, but straightening out Kirsten seemed like it was probably going to be a lifetime proposition.

Right now, he had a bigger mission, something much more urgent.

He was going to give Kirsten the thing she believed she could not have. He was going to convince her that good could come from bad, and that love could be the final victor.

He stomped back over to the empty building. His real-estate agent, an old friend from high school, was waiting for him.

"I hate it when you get that look on your face," Ed said. "Mean. You always looked like that right before you creamed me on the football field. It's gotta be a woman."

"A difficult one," Michael snarled.

"You don't want the easy ones," Ed said wisely.

"Now you sound like my mother."

They entered the building with Ed's key.

The space they entered was musty and a mess. There was rubble on cold, concrete floors, the inner walls were filthy, the ceiling lights were broken. Still, Michael was pleasantly surprised by how structurally sound the building was. It still had original brick on some of the interior walls, the roof had not leaked, the wiring and plumbing seemed good.

"This is going to be the Grant Baker Reading Center,"

Michael said. Despite the mess, he could already see it. The bookshelves, bright walls, hardwood floors, refurbished brick, new lighting.

"The what?" Ed asked doubtfully.

"Kids are going to come here to read."

"That should be fun for them, as long as they don't have to play tug-o-war with the rats."

"Why am I surrounded by difficult people?" Michael muttered. "It's going to be all fixed up. New flooring, paint, lighting. I'm going to put in a fireplace over there, a kitchen right here."

He was asking for a Christmas miracle and he knew it. He wanted to find a way to give Kirsten back her heart.

"We're opening on Christmas Day," he told Ed, firmly.

For a single, astonishing moment Michael could see it as if it already was: a room filled with kids on pillows and looking through books and munching on apples. A room where hippos in tutus danced on the walls.

Michael knew that's what real gifts did. They gave endlessly and to everyone.

There was only one real gift.

He supposed it could come in different forms: it could come as a building transformed. Or as wildly inappropriate emerald earrings. It could come as a sleigh on Christmas Eve giving gifts to children who had none. Maybe it could even come as Smedley in shining armor. But no matter how the gift was packaged, there was only one real gift.

Love.

That was the gift that Christmas was all about. It was the power the wise men had followed when they followed the star, it was the voice a young woman had obeyed that had led her fearlessly to an uncertain future, to a baby being born in a manger. It was the message that a man had come to bring, and that was still being heard thousands of years later.

Love. Love one another. That simple, and that hard.

Kirsten left work late. Lulu insisted on walking her out to her car, wouldn't admit Michael had told her to.

Even hours later, Kirsten could *feel* his kiss on her, as if he had bruised her. Or branded her. Claimed her in some barbaric, primal—delicious—way. When he said he'd found a job, she was very sure he was just saying goodbyes, his excuse not to be here anymore, not to be around her anymore. But then the kiss: tender, forgiving, welcoming.

Or a goodbye kiss?

Exasperating, just like him!

She got in her car, and by pure chance, because it was not the way she always went home, she drove by the building she had once dreamed of buying.

A light shone from behind the windows. She could see a bright red Sold sticker had gone up over a For Sale sign that had been there so long it said "or ale" instead of for sale. When she slowed down, she could hear the sound of hammers.

She sped up, and felt sick.

That's what happened when you hesitated. That's what happened when you waited. Your dreams were stolen from you by someone who had the vision—and the fearlessness—to go forward. She had to quit waiting for life to come to her, waiting for every circumstance to be perfect before she was willing to make her move.

Michael had been right. Life wasn't perfect, except for Harriet and Smedley, frozen in glass. She wasn't even waiting for an elf anymore. So there weren't any elves available? What was she going to do? Wait for him to find her one? Depend on him?

Ha! She could be her own elf! She could wear a green suit and pass out presents. In fact, the idea filled her with such a rush of happiness she wondered how it was she had not thought of it before.

It was a message for her, though a hard way to learn it.

When she got home, she was phoning Michael. No more fear. If she wanted a knight in shining armor, she was going to have to make it very clear. She spoke English. She could not interpret this language of kisses and heated looks.

Well, yes she could, but she wanted his intentions—no, her intentions—confirmed in English.

He was available? Okay, then, so was she. She was going to take the biggest chance of her life. She was going to ignore the lessons she had learned from her mother and father, from James, from Becky and Kent, and do her best to believe that maybe happily-ever-after could still happen to her.

She was going to listen to the voice inside her that would not shut up: the one that said to her she *could* trust, *could* be courageous, *could* be open, *could* be vulnerable, *could* be worthy of a man like Michael.

If she was going to believe in miracles, why not hold out hope for Becky and Kent? How did she know that they might not get back together? What was a few thousand miles of separation if a miracle was meant to happen?

That's what she hated about Michael, who was willing to tackle Impossible Dreams and just about anything else he perceived as an obstacle head-on.

It made her *believe*.

Kirsten didn't even take off her jacket when she clomped across her floor in her boots. She didn't even glance at her beloved *Little in Love* collection, usually the first thing she did when she walked in the door.

She couldn't risk losing momentum.

Her fingers fumbled on the pages of the phone book. She found his number. What was she going to say?

But the new her was determined to be spontaneous! She was not going to plan *perfect* words, she was just going to let whatever she felt like saying spill out.

But his phone rang and rang.

He wasn't home. That familiar sick feeling welled up in her stomach. Had she lost him as surely as she had lost that building? Lost him because she had not trusted him with one little piece of herself?

"Hey, you've reached Michael. Leave a message, and I'll get back to you."

His voice ran across her spine like a touch. She felt flustered. She didn't know what to say after all, not even to a recording.

"Never mind the elf," she said in a rush, "I found one." And then she hung up and allowed herself to feel annoyed. That was her idea of a risk?

She called back, but felt the same moment of being paralyzed when the beep went off. "I forgot to leave my name. Kirsten. Just in case you are looking for elves for other people."

She slammed down the phone. What would the real risk be? To tell him the whole truth, that she loved him. Though after that garbled message, he could probably figure it out!

She sank down beside the phone, stared at it. Now there was the risk she was not ready to take. Oh, not the love part.

Somehow, without her permission, that part had already happened. That part was a done deal.

But to let him know?

Her face felt as if it was on fire. Her heart felt as if it was going to thud out of her chest. It didn't feel anything at all like the *Little in Love* figurines depicted it as feeling.

No, it felt rich and big and real. It felt as if it could tear her heart out of her chest and the breath from her body. No figurine was ever going to do that. It felt terrifying. And exhilarating. It felt like jumping off a cliff not knowing what was below, or how far you had to fall.

It felt like being alive.

It felt exactly as if she had slept, and was now awake, shaking off sleep, delighting in this second chance at being alive. It felt just as if she was a princess in a fairy tale, just as if she had been kissed back to life.

She wondered, suddenly, what he would be doing out at this time of night. Flustered, it occurred to her he might be with someone else.

She felt the wind leaving her sails, and felt angry with herself. No, no more *waiting*. If she wanted him, she was going for him, fighting for him, doing whatever it took.

Trusting him, a voice inside her whispered, the biggest step of all. She was trusting him. No, that wasn't quite it. She was trusting herself, to know a good man from a bad one.

She woke up the next morning to the sound of the phone ringing, leaped from bed, stubbed her toe in her hurry to answer, hoping it was him.

"Kirstie, it's me!"

Her sister sounding, well, jubilant.

"We're coming to spend Christmas with you. Grant and I."

"Really?"

"And—" slight pause "—I've got some great news. But it will keep. Don't worry about putting us up. I know how small your place is." Unspoken: and not wheelchair accessible. "We've booked a hotel."

Kirsten set down the phone and sank into a chair. Her sister was coming for Christmas. She didn't know how it was even possible. Money was always such a problem.

But she suspected how it was possible. *I've got some other great news.* Her sister had met a new man.

The sound in her sister's voice overshadowed the news that she was coming for Christmas.

It was over between Becky and Kent. They were never, ever getting back together.

As furious as she was at her brother-in-law, her ex-brother-in-law, hadn't she hoped that maybe this thing could be repaired? Hadn't some secret part of her hoped it could all be the way it was before?

See? She had allowed herself to *believe.* The part of herself that Kirsten was most afraid of was that she was a hopeless dreamer. How could that lead anywhere but to a broken heart? Her certainty of the night before—that she should stop waiting, and go after what she wanted, faded.

Seven days until Christmas...

"Do you want to see something cute?" Lulu asked. She put her finger to her lips and led Kirsten to the back room.

There, squeezed onto a spot on the back of the sleigh was Michael, fast asleep. He'd told Kirsten he had a job he had to do before Christmas. Urgent. Still, he managed to drop by here every night to see what they needed done. Kirsten wasn't entirely fooled. He didn't want her walking to her car by herself.

Which charmed her. Especially since he always took her hand, sometimes blew on it in that way that warmed, not just her hand, but her heart.

Twice, he'd followed her home and come in and played cards, but when she won she knew the poor guy was beyond exhaustion.

As she watched him sleep, she was overwhelmed with tenderness for him. She felt overwhelmed with longing. And she felt as much confusion as she had ever felt in her whole life.

She hated this roller coaster of emotion she was riding. She needed to know. She needed answers.

Taking a deep breath, she hiked up her skirt, climbed on the sleigh, squeezed into the tiny soft spot he had found.

And then she kissed him.

He woke up slowly, beautifully. She smiled at his groggy, grumpy expression, took his lips again.

And he answered her. His lips took hers, in quest. Searching. Both of them searching for a truth that was bigger than they were, bigger than all the pain they had been through, bigger than fairy tales.

She allowed herself to wonder what it would be like to wake up beside him each day of real life. It wouldn't be about ball gowns, or a maiden being rescued by a gallant knight on horseback.

What would it be about? Would they read the newspapers together in bed? Drink from a single coffee cup? Jump in leaves? Walk hand in hand? Burn the toast? Make babies?

The thought of those ordinary everyday moments caused

her to feel the most extraordinary warmth in her heart, the warmth that came with the certainty that she had found an everyday kind of prince.

A certainty that it would be good to always feel something this real.

"Hey," he said, and touched her cheek, "you're blushing."

"I know," she said. She didn't even try to think of fish. "That's what I do. I blush."

"Are you thinking naughty thoughts?" he teased.

"No!" She laughed. "Okay. Maybe."

He looked at her sleepily, as if he was watching the sun come up instead of her cheeks turn pink. Something flashed in his eyes...heated, sensual.

"This would be so much easier if you were a bad girl," he sighed.

"You could teach me. Look at how quickly I picked up on Ninety-Nine."

"Nope. Sorry. I'm turning over a new leaf. What time is it?"

She frowned. A moment like this shouldn't be followed by a question like that. *Time?* "It's just after midnight. Everyone has gone home," she said. Oh, goodness, did that sound like a blunt invitation to a more romantic moment? Necessary, since he seemed intent on being a gentleman, of all things! The blush deepened. He had to get it. But he didn't.

"After midnight?" The sleep chased from his face. He put her away from him, scrambled to sit up, ran a hand through his hair and got to his feet. "Hell, I've got to go."

Where did anyone have to go after midnight?

He paused, looked at her, smiled, warm and lazy and sexy. "Hard as it is," he said, "I've got to go, Kirsten." He leaned over and kissed her much too lightly, much too casually. There was regret in his eyes, but not enough to make him stay.

She watched him disappear, sat up crankily, clambered off the sleigh and smoothed the wrinkles out of another new dress, not one made for trysts on the back of a sleigh.

What she hated most about Michael Brewster was that she loved him enough to give fairy tales another chance.

Just a few short weeks ago, her life hadn't been like this: all topsy-turvy, her stomach doing a constant roller-coaster ride. Just a few weeks ago, everything had been predictable and she had been in control.

The problem with a man like Michael was that she was never going to be in charge of the script! Could she live with that?

She wasn't at all sure. But she was sure she could never go back to being content with what she had before. Never. And that's what she hated about love. It wrecked everything.

CHAPTER TEN

Christmas Eve...

MICHAEL BREWSTER felt drunk with exhaustion. Next time he wouldn't be quite so cocky about thinking he could make over an aging building that had been abandoned and neglected on such an impossibly tight time frame. He'd taken on a six-month job—and given himself about nine days to do it in.

Now it was crunch time. Still, it was almost done, a miracle of community spirit and generosity. As soon as the Santa Claus sleigh had delivered its cargo tonight, he'd get back over there and make sure the building was ready for its Christmas morning reveal to the neighborhood. And to Kirsten.

What humbled him were the volunteers who had gathered to make that reading center a reality for their community. They came slowly at first, and then in droves. Young men and young women too old for Santa. They came even though he could pay them nothing. They came even though he was becoming a tyrant who drove them to their limits.

His judgments about this neighborhood were smashed. These kids *wanted* desperately to work, they were eager to learn every skill he could teach them: tiling, plumbing, painting, carpentry, cement work—they shirked at nothing. Even the girls picked up sledgehammers and circular saws without hesitation and without complaint. Still, things took more time when the labor was eager but unskilled.

But the strangest thing of all had happened. The Grant Baker Reading Center had started as a gift to someone else.

A gift for Kirstie. A gift to give her back her trust in life, a gift that tried to tell her if people kept their spirits strong, they could make good come from bad.

But somehow it had become so much more. It was a gift to each young person who came through that door asking nothing, giving everything he had to give.

But it was Michael himself who seemed to be receiving the greatest gift of all. He acknowledged his life had not come back to him the day he had been pulled from the sea. No, it had begun to come back to him when he had gone through the doors of the Secret Santa Society.

He had begun to breathe again, to laugh, to feel. He actually got cold. He'd had to buy a winter jacket, and have his furnace at the house serviced. All of those things proof that he lived, finally.

But living wasn't enough.

To go to a woman like Kirstie, with your heart in your hands, and ask her if she'd be willing to take the biggest chance of all, he realized he had to do something more than be just living.

Days away from a new year, he finally knew what his future held. Personally, he hoped it held a little house, and a beautiful gray-eyed woman and babies. He hoped it held Christmas mornings of kids getting up too early, and ripping paper and squealing with excitement and delight. He hoped it held moments when the last gift was the most important…

That was why this work he'd found became so important. It made him worthy in a way he had not been before.

The man he had been before had been easygoing and charming. He'd loved good times, tailgate parties, trips with his brother and the guys, football games, gatherings with his close-knit family. He had wanted nothing beyond what that world had given him, nothing beyond his own contentment. His world had been, frankly and unapologetically, all about him.

He had been allergic to the word commitment.

And then along came Kirstie, his polar opposite in so many ways. Her whole world was about others, helping, changing the world, trying to make it safe, filling dark corners with love even while she tried to convince herself she did not believe in love.

Somewhere along the way she had forgotten she had her own needs and desires. She had become afraid to even ask.

She needed to become more selfish, he needed to become more selfless. The work he was doing now made him feel worthy of the love of that woman, worthy to become a father who would teach his children to be citizens of a bigger world.

He had stumbled onto a way to be more than he was before tragedy had touched him with his icy fingers.

The opening of the Grant Baker Reading Center tomorrow was only the very beginning. He was going to use some more of that money—insurance money, crab money, money from his parents' assets and his brother's—all that money that had become his when he had survived them. Finally the money was a blessing instead of a curse, finally he knew exactly how to use it.

Not for plasma televisions or cars or clothes or trips or a fridge filled to the brim with beer.

Something bigger. He was going to buy the vacant building

across the street from this one. It looked to be in even worse shape, which was a good thing when you were teaching young people how to tear something down, and then how to build it back up. A lovely irony that in the process, these kids, who had been torn down by poverty and lack of opportunity and poor education, were also built back up.

That new building would become The Brewster Family Memorial Skills Training center, and these young people so full of restlessness and dreams were going to learn everything he could teach them. The things he didn't know about, he would bring in others to teach. He had found out in the last two weeks he was a surprisingly good teacher—particularly with people so surprisingly eager to learn.

But all that was the future.

Right now, he had a different job to do. He just wasn't sure what it was. A crowd of volunteers was in front of the Secret Santa Society office, loading the last of the gifts onto the flat deck sleigh. Lulu was settling her bulk in Santa's chair. Kirsten had asked him to meet her here, told him she *needed* him, that he would have the most important job of the evening.

But where was Kirsten? Then his mouth fell open.

Since when had elves looked like that? They were supposed to be small and green and grumpy!

Kirsten came out the Secret Santa Society door in an elf costume that ended midthigh. Her legs, in bright green tights, looked like they went on forever. The outfit, which on closer inspection was a plain burlap sack, dyed and belted in the middle, was absolutely the sexiest thing he'd ever seen her wear, up to and including that magnificent red dress.

Kirsten Morrison looked like she had been born to be Santa's elf.

And wasn't that what she was? The person who did all the work behind the magic, the person who would be back at it on January 3, when everybody else was content not to think about Christmas for another year.

She was the one who glued it all together.

"There you are," she said, and came bustling over. "Here. Quick. Go get changed."

"I've been missing you," he said.

Ah, the beginning of that little blush.

"I look horrible," she said, "Don't look at me like that!"

"Like what?" He folded his arms over his chest, leaned back, looked at her like *that* even harder.

"You know."

"No, I don't."

"Like you're going to take me behind the building and ravage me," she whispered.

He realized he couldn't hide one single thing about how he felt about her. "That's exactly what I want to do," he said.

"What kind of person wants to ravage a frog?" she asked, then grinned. "Oh, I know, another frog!"

Suspiciously he looked in the bag she had handed him. An elf costume. Extra large!

"I'm not wearing tights!" he said.

"I couldn't find any to fit you. Be a sport. Remember that first day, Michael? You said you'd be an elf."

"A guy will say anything when he's trying to win the girl. Do anything."

"Oh, goodie, go get changed!"

He sighed, called to Lulu, "Hey, strike up the ravaging music. It's Good to be Green."

He wanted to wait until tomorrow to make this declaration,

but she was just showing too much leg. His legendary discipline evaporated.

"Froggie," he said, "I have to tell you something. I love you."

There it was out. Her face turned the same color as Lulu's suit.

He snagged her wrist, and pulled her close to him. He kissed her. And she kissed back.

He came up for air because all the volunteers were clapping and stamping their feet and catcalling.

He bowed. She stepped back from him. Unless he was mistaken her face was a shade or two darker than the Santa suit now.

"Behave," she growled without an ounce of conviction. "There's my sister and nephew."

"Uh-hmm."

"This is my sister, Becky," she said. "Becky, Michael."

Becky was also dressed in one of the green elf outfits, though she looked like she was being much more sporting about it than her sister. The two sisters were very much alike in looks, though Becky was obviously the more outgoing of the two, and it showed, even though they were dressed identically.

Becky took his hand, did not let on once that he had arranged her tickets and accommodations for her. Her eyes met his, full of knowing. She *knew* he loved her sister. Why did her sister have to be so difficult?

Because that's the way she was. Difficult, challenging, the kind of complicated girl a guy could spend the next hundred or so years with and never stop being surprised.

He bet, when she was ninety, he'd still be able to make her blush.

There was a whirring sound, an electric wheelchair.

"And this is my nephew, Grant. Now, quick, go get changed."

Michael shook Grant's hand, and then hustled off to get changed. The outfit wasn't nearly as bad as she could have made it: just a green sack that fit over his regular shirt and jeans, and a green hat with fur—but he didn't think it made him look much like an elf!

He looked at himself in the mirror and smiled. The things a man would do for love. Not just love of her, but a larger love, a love of his community, a love for his neighbors, even the ones he did not know by name and had never met.

A moment later, he boarded the sleigh, and realized he would not have missed this for the world, this moment when all those months, weeks, hours, minutes of hard work and planning paid off.

This moment when Kirsten became an emissary of pure love. He had never seen her quite like this: *shining* with joy and purpose, as if the holiness of the season had chosen to arrive through her. She may not have been playing Santa, but she *was* Santa—she perfectly personified the spirit of the season, healing coming from hardship and love triumphing over transgression.

This had all been rehearsed and double rehearsed. Santa read the name, the elves went into the huge storage bins on the flat deck that were organized by street, and handed the parcels down to volunteers who delivered them to the eagerly waiting children who lined the streets.

The streets, normally so empty looking and desolate were filling up with children and their families—mothers, grandmothers, aunts, uncles, fathers, grandfathers, sisters, brothers.

The streets had been cleaned of snow, so Grant was able to be part of the system that got packages from the sleigh to the curbside.

In the crowd, Michael saw the same miracle that he saw in Kirsten's shining face. He saw tears mixed with smiles. He listened to the shrieks of children as Santa called their names, the looks of wonder and hope on small faces as they looked at those wrapped packages, hugged them to themselves in anticipation of tomorrow morning.

Amanda Watson's name was called near the beginning. She was tiny for six, her hair lovingly done in beautiful corn rows. Her eyes opened very wide when her name was called by Santa.

Michael found her huge box, jumped off the sleigh to deliver it personally. The tiny girl stared. Her hand crept into the young man's beside her. She turned and looked up at him, said in a tiny, disbelieving voice, "For me?"

She didn't have a hope of lifting it but luckily the man she was with—an older brother or an uncle whom Michael recognized as one of the young men who had come to work every day—lifted the box easily to his shoulder. That young man's gaze locked on Michael. The little girl was dancing around him, tugging on his free hand and squealing, and yet he remained still.

Of all the special moments of that night, Michael thought maybe he would remember that one the most— gratitude and dignity, mixed, a feeling of being one with another person.

The young man mouthed words. Thank you.

And Michael knew that somehow, he, too, had become worthy of carrying the spirit of Santa within him.

Finally the sleigh was back in front of the Secret Santa Society office, the volunteers, elves, even Santa, strangely quiet, contemplative, in that rare place of people who had been allowed the grave honor of being a part of something bigger than themselves.

Lulu took the microphone one last time. "Oh, wait. Santa has a few things left in his sack."

In a way this was Michael's moment. The moment he had been making secret lists for, the mission that had returned his heart to him.

And yet he could not stay for it. It wasn't about him, after all. To take credit for the work of Santa would have spoiled it all.

Michael walked away before she gave out those items, the Secret Santa gifts for each of the volunteers.

He walked away because his heart felt so big it hurt.

And because he had at least fourteen hours of work to do before tomorrow morning and only ten hours to do it in.

Because in each of those parcels they'd delivered tonight, had been an invitation to come to the Christmas Day unveiling of a surprise for the whole neighborhood.

Final coats of paint, furniture to be taken out of boxes and wrappers, last minute donations of books to be put on shelves, tiles to be grouted, Japanese oranges to be heaped in bowls.

He shoved his hands in his pockets and kept walking.

Lulu had left the mike on.

"Lord have Mercy," she screamed, "I'm gonna go get my feet pedicured in Air-ee-zona! And if I ain't going there in designer shoes!"

Kirsten watched as each of the volunteers accepted their gifts, was as stunned as anyone by the generosity and grandeur of those gifts.

Even her sister's name was called, and Grant's.

Grant had made a remarkable adjustment to being in a

wheelchair. Earlier today, Becky had seen Kirsten watching him and said, "You have to let go of your fantasy of who you thought he should be and see what he is, a kid with enormous heart and enormous spirit who would never let something like losing the use of his legs defeat him. He may have found that spirit if the accident had never happened. Or maybe not. You have to trust everything has a reason."

For four years now, Kirsten had focused on what wasn't, instead of what was. She had longed for happily-ever-after. But had it made her miss opportunities to be happy right now?

And trust? Everyone else had moved on. Everyone else had managed to accept life as it was, instead of as they wanted it to be.

Her sister was happy. Grant was happy. Everyone had chosen happiness, except her.

She was drawn back to the moment as Lulu called Grant's name, and passed her a basketball to give to him.

"Signed by some of the team," Lulu pointed out with approval.

But as Kirsten handed her nephew the basketball, something inside her froze. How could Grant and her sister be getting gifts? Who, aside from her, had even known they were coming? And who would have known about the interest in basketball? She hadn't even known that!

But suddenly, even as her own name was called, she knew who it was. She looked around for him, needing to see him, needing to see his eyes, and connect with them, needing to know he was *real*.

And needing him to know her final truth: she trusted him with her heart.

But like Santa, he had left his gifts and disappeared.

She took the parcel Lulu handed to her, and stared at it. Tonight, Michael Brewster had said the most incredible words to her.

He had said *I love you*. Whatever was in this beautifully wrapped parcel would tell her if it was true or not.

"Open it!" her volunteers called. They began to chant and clap. Kirsten opened the package with shaking hands.

Impossibly she was looking at the very distinctive box of a *Little in Love* collectible. Not just any *Little in Love* collectible, either.

How could he have managed this? She wasn't a Special Collector. Michael Brewster certainly wasn't a Special Collector. How had he managed to find her *Knight in Shining Armor*? It had sold out ten hours after it was issued.

And how is it when she was holding the item she had coveted the most, she felt a little worm of disappointment in her heart? What had she wanted from him? It was a beautiful gift, a gift that said he was willing to accept her even if her tastes ran contrary to his.

But the thing was, he had never accepted this part of her. It had always felt as if Michael saw more, expected more, made her become more. He had never accepted the comfortable smoke screens she hid behind. He had never seemed to see them at all. He'd seen right past them, to who she really was, to who she wanted to be.

Everyone was oohhing and aahing over her gift, knowing what *A Little in Love* had meant to her.

She tried to smile though the truth was her disappointment was so huge it felt as if she was going to burst into tears.

What right did she have to judge when the gift she'd gotten him didn't feel as if it began to say what she was feeling, either? She'd gotten him dance lessons, and at the last minute an MP3 player specially loaded with songs she'd selected. She'd gotten him fudge, and in a move so daring it made her blush thinking about it, she'd gotten him Christmas underwear that said, Oh, Oh, Oh, on it, instead of Ho, Ho, Ho.

Her sister came up beside her, looked at Kirsten's gift and made no effort to disguise her disgust.

"Good grief, Kirsten," Becky said, "Have I ever told you how much I hate those things?"

"You hate *Little in Love*?" Kirsten asked, shocked.

"You can't see why?"

Kirsten looked at the picture on the box she held. Of two people who loved each other blissfully, innocently. What was to hate about that?

Her sister shook her head. "Smedley looks exactly like Kent."

Kirsten stared at the picture on the box, stunned. How on earth had she managed to miss that? And yet nothing could be truer. Smedley did look like Kent.

With trembling fingers she opened the box, and carefully tugged the figurine from its specially made bed of foam and bubble wrap.

Kent in the form of Smedley stared her in the face. She slid a look to her sister, who was throwing the basketball to Grant.

The only one who was holding out hope that she would get back with Kent was Kirsten. The hope died in her. It was over. They were never getting back together.

"Hey, Mom, catch." Grant let loose the ball, but the throw went wild.

Becky leaned to catch it, and lost her footing. She screamed, trying to warn her, but Kirsten looked up a fraction of a second too late. Her sister crashed into her full force.

Later, when she looked back at it, it seemed to her when her sister fell into her, she could have held on to Harriet and Smedley much, much tighter.

But she chose to let go.

She chose to save herself instead. The figurine flew out of her hands, popped up in the air, eluded Mr. Temple's wild grab for it, and crashed to the ground.

The sound of splintering bisque porcelain was surprisingly loud in the sudden silence.

Kirsten stared down at the shattered glass. She became aware everyone was watching her. Grant looked like he was going to start crying.

But Kirsten got it, entirely.

The fantasy was done, shattered beyond repair. Right now, standing there, looking at that broken piece of glass, Kirsten was aware she had a choice to make. This could be her worst Christmas ever, knowing that her sister was moving on, knowing that things shattered unexpectedly and without warning, and could not be repaired.

Or it could be her best Christmas ever. She had a choice to make about how she intended to live.

The fantasy was gone, and rather than being sad, she decided to be glad. She could not remember one moment in the past four years when she had felt like this: free.

Free. Light. Ready.

To accept reality, which was about a man who hated dressing up, and fell asleep on the back of the sleigh, and disappeared when it could have been his moment to shine, his moment to lap up glory and gratitude.

Reality was a man who looked equally happy to see her dressed up as a princess, or as an elf. Reality was a man who delighted in making her turn the exact same shade as a fall-harvested beet.

Reality was a man whose eyes could turn her insides to jelly, whose hands lit fires within her, whose lips made her want to find out what it was to be a woman. Not a princess, but a 100 percent flesh and blood woman.

A woman every bit as real as he was. She recognized the saddest truth about herself: for the past four years she had been afraid of love, and equally afraid of not being loved. Smedley had been something safe for her to love.

Michael had seen right through those things, before she had even seen through them herself. He had made her long to find her courage so that she could love someone real.

You could look so hard for your knight in shining armor that you could miss what had been put right in front of you.

The lightness filled her. As she let go of her fantasy, she remembered the faces of each of the children she had handed a gift to tonight.

And allowed herself to feel—as she had not felt in four years—all their joy and all their pain, all their hopes and all their dreams.

Kirsten began to laugh, and as the clock struck midnight, Washington Street greeted Christmas with the sound of laughter—the hope and joy of helping others—rising above all other things.

"Can you find your own way back to the hotel?" Kirsten asked her sister. "I have to find Michael."

CHAPTER ELEVEN

Christmas Day...12:10 a.m.

THE door squeaked open, and Michael looked up. Lulu waltzed in, grabbed him and nearly crushed him in her hug.

"You should have stayed," she admonished him. "People figured out it was you. They just wanted to thank you."

"They can thank me tomorrow." Casually he added, "Did Kirsten like her present?"

"It got broke."

"What?"

"Yeah, her nephew was fooling around with a basketball. His mom tried to catch it and crashed into her. It got broken." Lulu passed him the box. "I picked up the pieces. Just in case you bought it with your credit card. Sometimes they'll replace things."

"How did Kirsten react?" He took the box, knew he was never having this replaced.

"She laughed."

Despite the fact that stupid figurine had been practically paid for in blood, Michael felt a sigh within himself. She had laughed at the smashing of Smedley. He bet when he was ninety, she would still be surprising him.

"Hey," he called to a boy who came in the door, a wizard with murals, "do you think you could paint this on the wall? The picture on this box?"

The kid was thrilled to have more to do.

As he began his task another young man, Malcolm, slipped in the door. "Got something for me to do, boss?" he asked.

Michael could ask a lot of himself, but he didn't hold everyone to the same standard. He had no one to go home to. Most of these guys did.

"It's Christmas Eve, go home and be with your family."

"Christmas," Malcolm corrected him. "It's been Christmas for like fifteen minutes." Then he grinned. "You are my family now."

The door opened again.

"Barney," he said sternly, "your mother wants you at midnight mass."

But Barney shook his head, stubbornly. "I'm finishing what I started."

Lulu kissed him right on the mouth. "I always wanted to kiss Santa," she said, "Now point me at the cleaning supplies, and I'll get at these windows."

The door opened again and again, and again, his "crew"—no, his family—coming to be with him.

"There's probably better things to be doing Christmas morning than grouting tile," he said, but not one of them moved. "Okay, but let's hope we're not starting a new Christmas tradition. Gather around guys and gals. Grouting 101."

Christmas Day 1:00 a.m.

In the distance Kirsten heard a church bell ringing, midnight mass ending. Where was Michael? How could she have let him disappear?

She had been making this all about her. Her family was here because of Michael. Even the Christmas present, and her disappointment that it had fallen so far from the mark about how she wanted to feel, had been about her. Somehow, because she loved him, Michael was supposed to make her feel good and secure and loved? And what had she done for him?

He, who had made Christmas magic for every single volunteer at the Secret Santa Society. Who had brought her sister and Grant here.

How had she thanked him? She'd left him alone!

It was his first Christmas by himself, and she had been so involved in herself she hadn't even thought how that must feel for him.

She realized that that was one of the things she was going to love about being in love. People might think she was unselfish, because of the work she did, but she was the most self-centered person of all. Everything was always about how *she* felt, even making sure she got presents to those kids. It made her feel in control, as if she could prevent tragedies like the one that had taken Grant's ability to walk.

She wanted respite from it. She was ready to grow beyond it. That's what love did: it required her to be so much more than she ever had been before.

She didn't know exactly where Michael's house was, but she did know where Mr. Theodore lived, because book club rotated through all the members' houses. Michael had said they were neighbors.

She drove there at the speed of light. Mr. Theodore's house was lit up in a display that would have put the Fourth of July to shame.

All the houses on the street were lit up.

Save for one. No lights. Dark. Very sad looking. She would have known it was Michael's house even if there wasn't a sign on the gate that said Brewster.

He'd given everyone else including her everything they dreamed of for Christmas, and she'd allowed him to come home, alone, to this.

She took a deep breath, tried to pull her elf costume a little farther down her thigh, and went and knocked on the door. No answer. She rang the bell. Still no answer. She stood on tiptoe and looked in the window high up the door. "Michael!" she called.

"Kirsten?"

She nearly jumped out of her skin. "Oh, Mr. Theodore, what are you doing out here? It's the middle of the night." The old man was standing on the walkway behind her. He was holding a bundle of something. Surely not a baby?

"I was just about to ask you the same thing. Michael's not here. He hasn't come home yet. He parks right out front."

Disappointment stabbed at her, but even as it did she discovered something else she loved about love.

Two months ago if she had come to a man's house in the middle of the night and he wasn't home, she would have thought of Kent, and she would have believed the worst. But Michael had leaned close to her tonight and told her he loved her. And he hadn't been kidding, even if he had called her a frog. He'd worn an elf suit for her, and if that wasn't love, nothing was!

She had decided tonight that was the gift she was giving herself: she was trusting again.

"Do you know where Michael might be?" she asked. "I'm worried. His first Christmas without them. I don't want him to be alone."

"I think this would be the hardest place for him to come tonight," Mr. Theodore said. "They always had a big party on Christmas Eve. His mother loved Christmas. She was a wonderful woman."

"She had to be to raise a man like him," Kirsten said.

"Ah," Mr. Theodore said, watching her with satisfaction. "Eileen would have had this place looking different. We used to compete good-naturedly to see who could put out the best display. I don't even think Michael has a tree."

Kirsten moved from the door, put her hand to the window to peer in.

Mr. Theodore was right. There was no tree. Not a single Christmas decoration. In fact, she was looking at just about the loneliest room she had ever seen. A big armchair and a huge TV set appeared to be the only furnishings in his living room.

"Oh, Mr. Theodore," she said sadly.

"Come, dear, we'll put the babe in the manger together."

"The babe?"

He gently jiggled the bundle he was carrying. "I usually put Him out as soon as midnight strikes, but I'm getting old. I slept. I think the sound of your car arriving is what woke me."

On that silent street, Mr. Theodore led the way to his lean-to stable. In it were life-size plywood replicas of Mary and Joseph. There was even a donkey.

Kirsten watched as Mr. Theodore tenderly lay the baby in the empty manger.

It wasn't a real baby. It was a child's doll wrapped in a blanket.

And yet when he laid that baby down so tenderly, she felt everything that baby had come to stand for being born within her.

It occurred to her, in a moment of illumination, that the world was rarely changed in meaningful or lasting ways by princes and princesses, by kings and queens, by celebrities with their star status.

No, the world was changed by ordinary men and women. It was changed by carpenters and fishermen, by housewives and caregivers, simple people who made a choice to rise above the ordinary by accepting the challenge of love.

No, it was not always storybook love, not always wine and roses and gowns and gifts. Sometimes, it would be better than that, stronger, more real, more resilient.

It would be love that forgave the argument. Love that found patience after the baby cried all night. Love that rose, strong and triumphant, above tragedy, above betrayal, above trial, above tribulation.

That was the true gift of the season: a rebirth of faith, hope, charity. And love. Yes, especially love.

"I wonder if I could find a tree at this time of night?" she pondered out loud.

"There's a lot at the end of the street. They won't be selling any more trees. I have a key to his door somewhere. For emergencies, which I'm sure this qualifies as."

The Christmas tree lot was deserted, and Kirsten walked around it guiltily. She chose the best one that was left. She was probably going to get arrested.

She giggled at the thought of getting arrested in her Santa's elf costume stealing a Christmas tree.

A month and a half ago it would not have been even a possibility in her well-ordered life.

And that's what she loved about love. It took a well-ordered life and turned it topsy-turvy.

She figured if she was stealing a tree, it might as well be a good one.

The plan took hold. She would fill his house with love: a tree, decorations. Maybe they could have the Christmas turkey there with her sister's family! Michael would know how to quickly build a ramp. She somehow managed to get the tree loaded into her car—it kept falling off the roof so she stuffed it in the hatchback.

When she got back to Michael's the lights were on and Mr. Theodore had made himself at home inside, putting hot chocolate on the stove. Michael's kitchen didn't look as if anyone had cooked anything here for a long time. Kirsten walked around looking at the walls, the whole history of Michael's family up there. She felt as if she could feel love gathering around her.

"I brought a few things from my own house," Mr. Theodore said. "He didn't even have milk in his fridge."

Kirsten went and peeked in his fridge. It was nearly as sad a sight as no Christmas tree. All that time he'd spent making Christmas so special for everyone else, and he didn't even have a stick of butter in his fridge.

"I brought a few other things, too." A few things were boxes and boxes of decorations and garlands and candles. The two of them worked side by side until the house looked and smelled of Christmas. Mr. Theodore looked around and sighed.

"I think he's going to make it, Kirsten. There have been times I doubted."

"Why me?" she said. "Why did you send him to me? How did you know I was the one in worse pain than him?"

Mr. Theodore looked startled. "My dear, I didn't know that. I sent him to help the children who needed presents. Speaking of presents, there's nothing under the tree. I'll be right back."

She went and got the gifts she had purchased for Michael and put them under the tree. Mr. Theodore came back. In his hand was a framed photograph.

"I took this," he said, "Right before they left for Alaska for the last time."

He gave it to her. It showed a happy family, in front of this very house. Michael, his brother who was slightly shorter than him, older, but who had a look of mischief on his face, and merriment. The look was repeated in the father's face. His mother looked so contented.

Kirsten's own mother often said people ended up with the faces they deserved, and when Kirsten looked at Michael's mother she saw a face of gentleness and strength, a face that radiated the happiness of a woman who was loved by the men in her life.

Not knights in shining armor, not one of them.

And yet each of them, something in their body language so fiercely protective of her, so fiercely loving, that Kirsten knew, even though they didn't wear the costumes, even though they probably had not been chivalrous, but had left their socks on the floor and their crumbs on the counter, these men had been her knights.

She ran her fingers tenderly over the face of the woman she

would only meet through her son, and went and placed the picture under the Christmas tree.

As a last touch, she lit luminaries—candles inside white waxed bags—and placed them on the walk so Michael could find his way home.

When all was done, Mr. Theodore wished her a Merry Christmas and left.

She curled up in Michael's big chair, amazed that it could look so ugly and be so comfortable, and before she knew it she slept.

The next thing she knew, her cell phone was ringing.

"Kirsten," her sister sounded panicked, "where are you?"

She shook herself awake. Morning light painted the Christmas tree gold. She was at Michael's. He had never come home? Was he okay?

"Do you know where Michael is?" she asked without answering her sister's question.

There was a pause. "Darling girl," her sister said gently, "if you fall any more in love with that man, I think we'll just cancel Christmas, because it can't even compete with the show the two of you are putting on."

Christmas! She was supposed to have gone to the hotel this morning to open gifts. But that didn't even seem important.

"Do you know where Michael is?" she repeated. That poor man. Choosing to be all alone Christmas Eve, now Christmas Day. She had to find him. She had to let him know what she had found out.

That was what she loved about love. You wanted to share your whole world with another person, no secrets.

"I do know where Michael is," her sister said. "I have orders to bring you to him. Can you meet me here?"

Kirsten was still dressed like an elf, and she didn't care.

She ran out past the luminaries that had burned to puddles of wax during the night. She was at the hotel in less than five minutes.

"Turn around," her sister ordered, when she arrived "and be quick about it. I'm going to be in so much trouble if we're late."

"But I don't want any more surprises from him. It's my turn!"

"Just shut up and enjoy it," her sister said, and then muttered, "while it lasts."

"A blindfold? Are you kidding?" Apparently she wasn't.

She was put back in her car, her sister drove this time. She still felt giddy. Imagine if they got pulled over now. How were they going to explain kidnapping an elf on Christmas Day?

The car stopped. Kirsten could hear a whole lot of people, feel the chill of the morning on her cheeks.

And then she felt his lips and smelled his smell.

"Ah," he said, "Santa's favorite little elf."

"What are you up to?"

He tugged the blindfold up, and for a moment all she could see was his eyes.

They were not the eyes of a man who had wandered away Christmas Eve in loneliness and despair.

"I have a gift for you," he said.

"You've given me enough—"

He put his finger to his lips, touched her shoulder, turned her around.

She turned. They were just around the corner from Washington Street. The street was nearly as full as it had been last night, even though it was Christmas Day. Many of the children were wearing brand-new coats. The smaller ones clung to new bears, the older ones had MP3 headphone wires dangling from their ears.

She saw she was staring at the building that had sold out from under her, before she had a chance to realize her dream for it.

It was completely refurbished. A sign hung above it, covered with a piece of canvas.

"Grant," he said, "Pull the cord."

Grant pulled the cord, and the canvas floated down over the street. Children laughed and ducked out of the way.

She read what had been revealed.

"The Grant Baker Reading Center."

Grant was doing wheelies up and down the street. "Whoo-eee," he yelled. "A building named after me."

Her legs felt as if they were falling out from under her, but Michael was right there propping her up.

"You want to see what's inside?" he asked in her ear.

All she could do was nod. He led her across the street. The doors opened.

Inside was heaven. Shelves of books, soft lights, wooden floors, rich area rugs, colorful pillows. The children were coming in behind her, like a river flowing around a rock. Soon the space was filled with them, reaching for books, finding a place to sit.

She looked at the walls, and gasped. They were the best of all. A whimsical hippo danced in a pink tutu. A mouse was passed out near a moon made of cheese. Sleeping Beauty's castle was surrounded by a moat.

And there, in front of it, was Smedley, six feet high, riding his white horse, bending down to kiss Harriet's hand. Only Smedley didn't really look like Smedley. He looked like Michael. And Harriet looked like her!

"That's the closest I'm ever getting to being a knight," Michael said.

She just smiled, because she knew a different truth. True

knights carried their strength and integrity inside of them, and then, for one special, very lucky person, they took the armor off, their heart exposed.

She whispered a goodbye to her sister and Grant, and turned to Michael.

"Now," she said, "Michael, now it's your turn. It's time for us to go home."

He was astounded when he saw his house, he became very quiet.

"Was it okay to do this, Michael?"

"More than okay," he said, took her and hugged her to him. Then she made him sit down and open his gifts. He laughed about the dancing lessons. They ate fudge for breakfast. He opened the package with the underwear, and didn't say one single word. He just stared at her until her face was glowing brighter than the star atop his tree.

Then he laughed. "That's what I wanted for Christmas. Kirstie's blush."

He put the earplugs of the MP3 player in his ears.

"You want to dance?" he asked.

"Yes." They had to dance very close to both be able to hear the player.

Then, finally, she brought him the lone photo from under the tree.

"From Mr. Theodore," she said.

Michael studied it, ran his hands across faces he would not see again in this lifetime.

Kirsten looked at his hands. From the first moment they had told her everything about who he was: the hands of a strong, capable man. Hands that could make a woman so, so aware she was alone, and make her long for a different reality.

Now she could see he had taken his armor off, for her. She could see his heart. A man strong enough to take the worst life has to offer and to allow it to make him better, stronger, wiser, instead of broken, bitter, angry.

He put the picture down, not under the tree, but on the mantel.

"Welcome home," she said softly.

"It's not home quite yet."

"No?" She looked around to see what had she left out of her decorating efforts.

His hands found her chin, brought her eyes back to his.

"You can give me the gift I want most of all right now," he said softly.

She knew what was coming.

"I want you to marry me, Kirstie. I want to have you to love, to give you the gift my family left me."

She could not even trust herself to speak. She nodded, and when she did he took her in his arms, kissed her, twirled around until her little green elf hat fell on the floor and she was blushing so hard it felt as though her face would catch fire.

"There it is," he said with satisfaction. "What I wanted most of all, not just for this Christmas. I want to make you blush forever. Welcome home, Kirstie."

HARLEQUIN Romance.

New York Times bestselling author

DIANA PALMER

Handsome, eligible ranch owner Stuart York knew
Ivy Conley was too young for him, so he closed his heart
to her and sent her away—despite the fireworks between
them. Now, years later, Ivy is determined not to be
treated like a little girl anymore…but for some reason,
Stuart is always fighting her battles for her. And safe in
Stuart's arms makes Ivy feel like a woman…his woman.

Winter Roses

Available November.

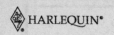

Every great love has a story to tell ™

Charlie fell in love with Rose Kaufman
before he even met her, through stories her
husband, Joe, used to tell. When Joe is killed
in the trenches, Charlie helps Rose through
her grief and they make a new life together.
But for Charlie, a question remains—can
love be as true the second time around?
Only one woman can answer that....

Look for

The Soldier and
the Rose

by
Linda Barrett

Available November wherever you buy books.

HEL65421

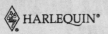

REQUEST YOUR FREE BOOKS!

2 FREE NOVELS PLUS 2
FREE GIFTS!

HARLEQUIN ROMANCE®

From the Heart, For the Heart

YES! Please send me 2 FREE Harlequin Romance® novels and my 2 FREE gifts. After receiving them, if I don't wish to receive any more books, I can return the shipping statement marked "cancel." If I don't cancel, I will receive 4 brand-new novels every month and be billed just $3.57 per book in the U.S., or $4.05 per book in Canada, plus 25¢ shipping and handling per book and applicable taxes, if any*. That's a savings of over 15% off the cover price! I understand that accepting the 2 free books and gifts places me under no obligation to buy anything. I can always return a shipment and cancel at any time. Even if I never buy another book from Harlequin, the two free books and gifts are mine to keep forever.

114 HDN EEV7 314 HDN EEWK

Name _____ (PLEASE PRINT) _____

Address _____ Apt. _____

City _____ State/Prov. _____ Zip/Postal Code _____

Signature (if under 18, a parent or guardian must sign) _____

Mail to the **Harlequin Reader Service®:**
IN U.S.A.: P.O. Box 1867, Buffalo, NY 14240-1867
IN CANADA: P.O. Box 609, Fort Erie, Ontario L2A 5X3

Not valid to current Harlequin Romance subscribers.

Want to try two free books from another line?
Call 1-800-873-8635 or visit www.morefreebooks.com.

* Terms and prices subject to change without notice. NY residents add applicable sales tax. Canadian residents will be charged applicable provincial taxes and GST. This offer is limited to one order per household. All orders subject to approval. Credit or debit balances in a customer's account(s) may be offset by any other outstanding balance owed by or to the customer. Please allow 4 to 6 weeks for delivery.

Your Privacy: Harlequin is committed to protecting your privacy. Our Privacy Policy is available online at www.eHarlequin.com or upon request from the Reader Service. From time to time we make our lists of customers available to reputable firms who may have a product or service of interest to you. If you would prefer we not share your name and address, please check here. ☐

I ♥ HARLEQUIN Presents~

BROUGHT TO YOU BY FANS OF
HARLEQUIN PRESENTS.

We are its editors and authors
and biggest fans—and we'd
love to hear from YOU!

Subscribe today to our online blog at
www.iheartpresents.com

Always passionate, always proud.

**The richest royal family in the world—
a family united by blood and passion,
torn apart by deceit and desire.**

Don't miss

THE TYCOON'S
PRINCESS BRIDE

by favorite Harlequin Romance author

Natasha Oakley!

Isabella can't be in the same room as Domenic Vincini
without wanting him! But if she gives in to temptation
she forfeits her chance of being queen...and will tie
Niroli to its sworn enemy!

This sparkling story is part of the fabulous
Royal House of Niroli series—available in
Harlequin Presents this month!

Available October wherever you buy books!

HARLEQUIN *Romance*

Coming Next Month

Fall in love with our ranchers, bosses and single dads in a month filled with mistletoe and magic, and where happy endings are guaranteed!

#3985 WINTER ROSES Diana Palmer
Long, Tall Texans
Rugged rancher Stuart has always been protective of innocent Ivy. Growing up and finding your place in the world is tough, but there's nowhere Ivy feels more like a woman than in Stuart's arms. A fantastic new book from an award-winning author.

#3986 THE COWBOY'S CHRISTMAS PROPOSAL Judy Christenberry
Mistletoe & Marriage
The first book in this festive duet that's sure to get you in the Christmas mood. Penny has just inherited her family ranch, but she has a problem... she doesn't know how to run it! Luckily, help is at hand in the form of Jake, the gorgeous cowboy next door....

#3987 APPOINTMENT AT THE ALTAR Jessica Hart
Bridegroom Boss
Free spirit Lucy doesn't like being told what to do, so when irresistible tycoon Guy challenges her to find a real job, she does—as Guy's assistant! Don't miss the second book in this wonderful duet.

#3988 THE BOSS'S DOUBLE TROUBLE TWINS Raye Morgan
9 to 5
Don't you just love surprises? Workaholic businessman Mitch gets a big one when new employee and old flame Darcy gives him news that will change his life—he's going to be a daddy, to twins!

#3989 CARING FOR HIS BABY Caroline Anderson
Heart to Heart
Everyone makes mistakes, and sometimes second chances can be even sweeter than the first time around. When Emily opens her door to Harry, the man who broke her heart years before, he is cradling a little baby in his arms. How can she resist?

#3990 MIRACLE ON CHRISTMAS EVE Shirley Jump
If you love this joyful season, don't miss single father C.J. struggling with newfound fatherhood, and yearning for a magical Christmas. Jessica's heart is quickly won by C.J.'s enchanting daughter, but what about the man himself?